Book One

The Kingdom of Imagination

Return of the Darkness

By: Anna Eads

First Edition 2018

First Book in the Series "Kingdom of Imagination"

Layout by Matthew Eads

Edited by Amy Ammons Garza

Interior Illustrations by R. Stewart Eads, Sr

Front & Back Cover Illustrations by Doreyl Ammons Cain

Publisher: Anna M. Eads

ISBN-13: 978-0692094815 (Custom Universal)
ISBN-10: 0692094814
BISAC: Fiction / Fantasy / General

Printed in the United States of America

For the Wild with All its Creatures

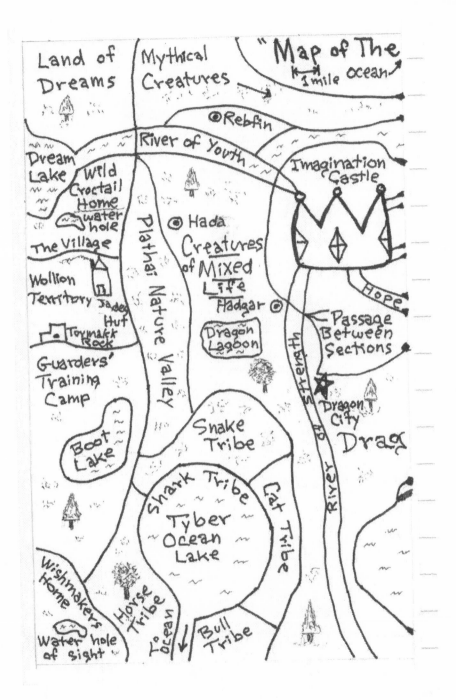

"Map of The ocean
1 mile

Land of Dreams

Mythical Creatures

Rebfin

River of Youth

Dream Lake

Wild Croctail Home
water hole

The Village

Imagination Castle

Hada

Creatures of Mixed Life

Hadgar

Wollion Territory   Jadeg Hut

Toymark Rock

Guarders' Training Camp

Dragon Lagoon

Hope

Passage Between Sections

Plathai Nature Valley

River of Strength

Dragon City

Drag

Boot Lake

Snake Tribe

Shark Tribe

Cat Tribe

Tyber Ocean Lake

River

Wishmakers Home

Horse Tribe

To Ocean

Bull Tribe

Water hole of sight

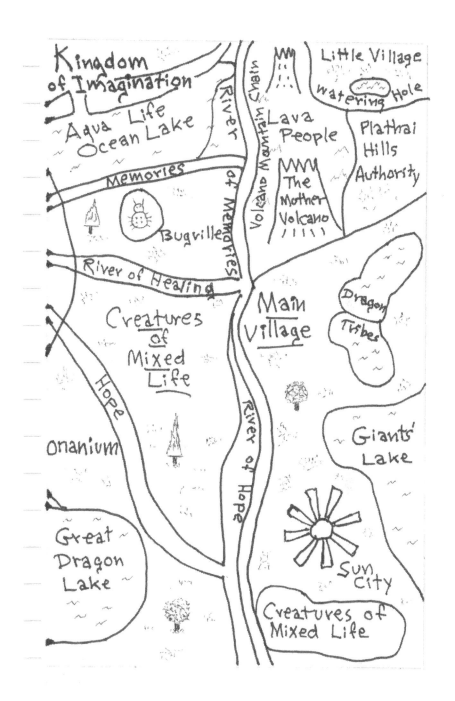

Contents

Prologue

Rain poured down on a rock sheltering a figure huddled beneath its strength. A strange sound—something alive—crashed through the forest. An inky blackness crept closer and closer. It was so dark, it made darkness darker. So close...one inch, another inch....

The darkness surrounded the figure. It compressed, choking the vague shape of a human. The human-figure gave a last, dying breath, then slumped against the rock.

Voices echoed through the forest. The patch of extreme darkness hissed, as if not wanting to be found by anyone. It fled into the night. It had not even been allowed enough time to kill its primary target because the other one had stood in the way. The dark spot hated when they did that. It was so annoying to get really close and then find out the target had moved to another galaxy.

Eyes appeared, looking into the small clearing. A flashlight let its beam rest upon the rock where the human-figure had sheltered from the pouring rain.

"What's out there?" asked a man. "Can you see anything, Jeb? Is it that weird thing we saw earlier?"

"Benny, I think I found something," another man whispered. "Keep quiet."

A soft sob whispered through the darkness, reaching the two men.

"That sounds like a..., " the first man, Benny, said.

"Baby," finished the second man, Jeb.

They crept forward, and the flashlight's beam fell onto the dark shape they had seen earlier. But now, they could see it more clearly.

The shape was a dead woman holding a baby.

Chapter One:
Taming the Most Vicious Creatures of All Time

With the invincible dome of golden thorns, and the Wild Croctail Dragons patrolling the entrances, the Kingdom of Imagination was quite well protected. But of course, Jade Skystone didn't know anything about the Kingdom—like the fact that the Kingdom was a realm coexisting with hers, and that the Kingdom was awaiting a new Queen.

Jade lay in bed on the orphanage floor. She had long, chestnut brown hair that matched her eyes. Around her neck was a little gold star necklace, the only thing that was from her parents. She didn't like to be fancy, and all the other girls at the orphanage teased her about her lack of fashion. But she didn't mind, at least not as long as they didn't steal her necklace and threaten not to give it back unless she stole some makeup.

Jade was thinking of her new nickname: Cheetah Jade. The orphanage girls were amazed at how fast she could get from one place to another. Jade's best and only friend, Lola, called her a cheetah because of how fast and strong she was, and good at hiding.

At recess, they played hide-and-seek tag. She was a natural at hiding, since her dull clothes and dark hair made her blend right in to her surroundings. As for running, she would tear through the playground. During PE, while playing swamp ball, Jade could hurl a foam ball forty feet and make it hit its target so hard the person would jump really high and scream like a baby.

She also liked myths and fantasy. Her favorite mythical creature was the Ridgeback Rattlesnake. The snake was a highly venomous rattlesnake which had a Mohawk-like ridge along the top of its head and along its back. Technically, the snake wasn't a mythical creature because there had never been a myth including it. But one night, she had a dream of the strange snake, including the name.

Jade also wanted very much to get adopted. She had already been to five foster homes so far, and they had all turned her down. The last one was a week ago, and it was the worst.

A family of a mom, a dad, and a son had agreed to foster her. The boy was really mean, and whenever his parents weren't around, he bullied Jade.

"Gimme that five-dollar bill you found on the street," he'd say. If she didn't give him the item he wanted, he would hit her.

One time, she lost her temper and punched him so hard he went flying out of the room, down the hallway, and into the next room, which turned out to be his parent's room. That ended her foster placement. Still, Jade wondered how he had flown that far. She hadn't punched him hard.

As she always did when she was thinking, Jade subconsciously turned the golden star necklace over and over with her fingers. It was the only treasure she had...the one connection she had to her parents.

A flash of silver, gold, and a little bit of purple outside the window of her closet-sized bedroom caught her attention. Two eyes blinked. The thing roared. Jade blinked and rubbed her eyes, so when she looked again, the object was gone. Funny! Jade could've sworn that she'd had a dream about something like that.

Try to get some sleep, she told her exhausted body. Then she collapsed onto her bed and went to sleep almost immediately, despite what she had just witnessed.

.   .   .   .   .

Suddenly Jade awoke, immediately crying out in astonishment. Before her was a swirling, gray portal cackling with lightning. Cautiously, she crept toward the portal. With a gasp, she realized there was a letter on the floor of her room. She picked it up, opened the rosefire seal, and read: *Step through the stormportal before it closes or else!*

The stormportal, or whatever, was already closing. By the time Jade made up her mind and launched herself into the portal, she landed with a thud onto the floor of the orphanage. Looking up, she saw the gray stormportal opening had closed.

Jade sat down on the wooden floor and thought. *Is this a trick?*

Maybe she was hallucinating. Most likely, it was a dream. She was going to wake up any minute and find herself still safe on the old, moth-eaten mattress that lay on her floor with nobody in her closet-sized room but her. Then she would hear the bell for breakfast, get up, and watch everyone stampeding towards the dining hall.

But, yet...there it was...a flash of silver, gold, and purple outside her window, just like the night before. Two eyes stared at her. Jade blinked and rubbed her eyes hard. When she looked again, the thing was still there. The object stared at her as if to say, *Open this window immediately or I bust down the whole building!*

Reaching her decision, Jade pushed open the rusty window with a loud *creeeeeeaaak.* The weathered dusty glass had made it hard to see through it, but when she opened the window, she could see what was staring at her.

It's a dragon!

A full-sized dragon glared at her, as if to say, *Hurry! We don't have all day!*

But the strangest part was not the huge body or the curved, glowing purple horns, but the fact the left half of its body was half golden and bright, like the sun, while the right glowed silver and dark, like the moon.

The dragon turned so his back was parallel to the wall. He looked back and snorted at her. Strangely, she had a feeling that he wanted her to get on.

Not even hesitating this time, Jade climbed onto the dragon. He spread his enormous wings and took off.

It was amazing, soaring over the little town of Healy. Soon, the streets of houses and stores disappeared, only to be replaced with vast mountains and beautiful valleys. Speeding up, Jade was forced to hunch behind the dragon's massive head to be protected from the cold, knife-sharp wind of Alaska.

The dragon seemed to be heading for Mount Denali, which would make an ideal lair for a dragon. According to the many books Jade had read, dragons liked mountains.

Morning turned colder for they had almost reached the summit of Mount Denali. *Everything* was colder when it was near the top of a mountain.

The dragon seemed to be saying something in English, but it was too hard to hear anything with all the wind rushing around them. For all Jade knew, he was talking to himself. But in English? Jade knew Dragons only spoke Dragonese.

Suddenly, another stormportal thing opened up in front of them, and they plunged straight into its crackling depths. It was a strange feeling; sort of like spinning, falling, and flying all rolled into one. Jade almost lost her dinner from last night.

As quickly as they had plunged in, the stormportal spat them out.

Landing beside the dragon, she looked up. She had to be hallucinating! Dragons, oversized birds, and other winged creatures soared through the open skies, while snake people slithered through the underbrush. Thousands of strange creatures chatted, walked, and apparently shopped.

The most beautiful thing of all, though, was the castle in the distance. Ruby walls and balls of light on top of spires made the castle spectacular. As soon as she laid eyes on it, Jade wanted to live there. Something inside her said, *Okay. Just walk into the castle and get a room.*

"If you prove yourself good enough, Imagination Castle is yours," said a deep, calming voice. The speaker seemed to be able to read her mind.

Jade looked around for the mystery voice. She found herself staring at the dragon that had brought her to this strange haven.

"I am the Dragon of the Sun and Moon. Walk with me. We have lots to talk about," said the dragon.

"Isn't there some other *shorter* name I can call you?" Jade asked the Dragon of the Sun and Moon.

"I am also known as Airgor...one of Lady Anivia's advisors," chuckled Airgor. "Anyway...about being worthy of the throne..., he began, paused, then continued, "Where to start? Oh, of course!"

He walked towards the woods, and Jade followed.

"Your friends have even noticed the power you have. Hurling a foam ball forty feet and making it hurt? That's not natural, you have the blood of the Royals flowing through your veins. The creatures here learn two languages: Imaginese and their own. Everyone can speak Imaginese, but you alone can hear and speak all the different languages of different species!"

"Well, then how come I've never spoken Imagine Geese before?" She asked, trying not to trip over rocks, for unlike the trees, they did not clear a path. It was as if the trees were alive and knew someone was coming.

"Imaginese! You haven't been face-to-face with any of the people who speak a different language," Airgor said quite plainly. "Here's some info in case you meet a basilisk. The basilisks here wear special sunglasses so they don't kill anyone, and their weakness is weasel stench. Basilisks have so much venom it leaves a trail of death wherever they go, so you can follow them to their hole. They can grow to be twelve finger-lengths long! Basilisks can kill you just by looking into your eyes. Their name means *little king* because of the crown on their heads. They live underground. Also, they have poisonous breath!" He gave her a dragonish grin as if this was his favorite creature in the world.

"Okaayyy," replied Jade. "Any other deadly creatures I should know about?"

"Not except for the ones you're about to meet."

They passed a pair of creatures that had the front legs of a lion, the hind legs of a rhino, a lion's tail and fur, a rhino's bulk and three horns, and a lion's face. The male had a mane. The female had nothing.

"What kind of creatures are those?" Jade wondered.

"Rhinolions," he grunted.

They walked on in silence, which took about forty minutes. As they walked, Jade looked around at all the creatures. There were centaurs with their back legs fused together to form a tail splashing in a pool, a dragon-like beast with a unicorn horn, three eyes, no wings, and a devil tail, and even a large bird with dragon wings and tail.

Airgor stopped abruptly. "We're here," he said.

"Umm...*here*?" Jade asked.

"Depends on what you mean. I'll go with what's here. This is a tribe of Wild Croctails' territory. We're right smack in the middle of the most terrifying creatures ever!" He gave her another dragonish grin. "Don't worry, you just have to check on this tribe once a day for a couple weeks. They'll give you directions to and from the hut they will lend you. All you have to do is check on them at sunset when you will attend to their ceremonies. After, you will listen to their needs and try to fix them. If you survive and not go "Wild Croctail," then the throne is yours," Airgor finished.

"Where are they?" Jade asked.

Airgor opened his huge mouth, as if going to respond, but instead let out a mighty roar. Somehow, she understood him perfectly: *"The heir to the throne has arrived! All shall come meet the future Chief! Treat her very nicely or I'll come kick your sorry butts!"* How he fit all of that into a single sound, Jade didn't know.

Airgor turned to her and said, "There. They shouldn't attack you now."

A noise behind Jade made her turn. A green, scaly creature was loping towards them. It had three curved horns in single file that got smaller as they got closer to the back of the head. The tail had two sets of curved spikes. The set closer to the tip of the tail was curved so that it could have held a soccer ball. The set slightly farther back could probably hold two soccer balls.

Three more arrived, then a younger one. Next came one with a greenish egg in the set of curved spikes closest to the tip of the tail.

The first Wild Croctail bared her fangs in a way that might have been a dragonish smile, though not like Airgor's. A green substance dripped from the fangs, causing the grass to vaporize into a tiny mountain of ashes.

An elderly looking Croctail with a ripped snout that seemed to be the leader stepped forward. "Welcome, heir of the throne," she said. "I am Chief Ripsnout. I need to talk with you privately. Then, Hooktail," she gestured towards a Wild Croctail with an unnaturally curved tail, "will guide you to a spare hut a little distance away. Come with me."

Jade followed Chief Ripsnout into a dark cave. As soon as she and Ripsnout walked in, though, hundreds of crystals lit up and made the dark cave not so dark.

"Our automatic mind-reading crystal light system," purred Chief Ripsnout. "Please, sit down and have a human-ka-bob!" She gestured towards a large plate filled with shish-ka-bobs.

Jade felt sick.

"Only joking, that is vegetable meat. Tastes like venison, made of plants! Now, every evening, at six o'clock on the dot, we have our ceremonies. Please come at 5 o'clock for dinner. The chefs make simply wonderful firecakes. At 7 o'clock, we will consult with you for guidance. Then you shall go back to your hut."

"Okay."

"Hooktail will give you directions."

"Okay."

"Come find me if you need anything."

"Okay."

"Hooktail will see you now."

"Okay."

Chief Ripsnout led her back outside, where Hooktail was waiting. "Come on," he said.

The forest was growing darker and darker as they traveled through the partly swampy terrain. At last, they reached a small wooden hut. Hooktail handed her a map. It was so detailed she could see every line on every leaf. It even zoomed in and out on command!

"Just follow the red line. Make sure you're on the trail by matching the map to the world," he explained. "It's a good idea to leave half an hour early, as the trail takes about that long. Also, there's a garden out back."

"I'll have to check that out! What food could I bring in tomorrow? Possibly some ghost peppers?" Jade absolutely loved ghost peppers.

"Yes, ghost peppers are good. Remember, 5 o'clock tomorrow for food, 6 o'clock for ceremonies, and 7 o'clock for guidance. Also, look out for Howler. He's a Wollion: half wolf, half lion. He is the worst creature in the forest, though some think he's a legend. I'm with the group who says he haunts the forest. They say he has eyes the color of the bluest diamonds," Hooktail replied. He waved his crooked tail back to the forest from which they had emerged. "I need to go. See you tomorrow!" He launched himself into the darkening sky.

Way to freak out a newcomer. Jade walked to the hut and opened the front door. There was a sudden flare and the mind-reading lights turned on. A bed lay in one corner while a book shelf sat in another. In the center of the room was an endless stone water fountain. An old wooden door led to the garden.

Suddenly, the bed looked wonderful, much better than her moth-eaten mattress at the orphanage. She was exhausted, since the trek through the forest had drained her. Laying down, she thought, *Sleep now. Explore tomorrow.* She just wished the lights would turn off. As if hearing her thoughts, the glowing crystals dimmed one by one.

As she lay down, she saw a pair of diamond-blue eyes glinting in the dark. Then, they disappeared. *It's probably just some bird outside,* she thought, closing her eyes.

And then claws gripped her throat.

"Who are you and what are you doing in my territory?" A huge shadow of what was speaking loomed above her. Jade could see the glinting of razor-sharp teeth a bit too close to her head.

"I-I am Ja-Jade, heir t-to the throne," she wheezed. The claws released her at once. Rubbing her bruised throat, she asked, "Who are *you*?" She wished that the crystal lights would turn back on, and they did.

Jade was staring at a large golden wolf.

Well, the wolf wasn't *completely* golden. His face had streaks of gray in it. His belly was white. The tuft of fur at the tip of his tail was black. He had what looked like a mane, but it wasn't like a lion. It was like the creature had a shield of furry spikes that were very close together. His gaze permanately looked like he was planning something mischievous.

He found her staring at him. "Sorry for disturbing you, Princess...I am a Wollion, the sacred animal of the goddess of the Kingdom of Imagination, Lady Anivia. My name is Howler."

Chapter Two:
The Big Not-So-Bad Wolf-Lion

Jade thought she looked brave enough to be convincing on the outside. But on the inside, she was trembling with fear. Her heart rate increased, she was sweating... All of which Howler could probably smell, being half wolf and all. *This was the creature Hooktail had told her about.*

Howler snorted. "If you are good at concealing your fear, then I'm a house cat. Also, I'm not what the stories say I am. The story that earned my reputation is simple: I got into a fight with my alpha, who was the biggest, most ferocious Wollion who ever lived. He was the size of a full-grown male lion, which is, like, ginormous for a Wollion. Anyway, he leaped onto me, so I clawed his belly. When he staggered off of me, I ripped out his windpipe. He died of his injuries a minute later. By Wollion law, I am the alpha. I'm still here because everyone is too afraid to challenge me."

"Scary!" Jade was not trusting this Howler.

"Yeah, a Wollion named Beast thought I was a monster and started the legend of Howler the Haunted. Thought it'd be funny if he told the local Croctails," Howler finished.

"Well," Jade said, now completely trusting him, "that does make sense." She yawned. "I really need to sleep. If you could come visit tomorrow around ten o'clock in the morning, then that would be wonderful. Maybe you could explain to me everything that's happened in the past hour."

Howler grinned. "Yeah, okay, it feels good to be wanted again. Hey, do you know how to read Imaginese yet? You have to be taught to read Imaginese."

"Uh, no."

Howler responded, "Well, I'll have to teach you."

"I'll be waiting. Don't forget, ten o'clock in the morning!"

"I also need to go. I'm hungry!"

Jade laughed. Still smiling, she waved at him as he disappeared into the dark forest in the night. Then, completely exhausted, she lay down and fell asleep.

.　.　.　.　.

When Jade woke, the sun was shining through her window. She glanced at the clock beside her bed. It was just after nine o'clock. Outside, the garden looked beautiful...she could see it through the window on the door.

She dressed and raided the pantry in twenty minutes flat. Walking through the door leading to the garden, she saw the morning mist was making the entire place glitter like Howler's diamond-blue eyes.

There were rows of trees and plants, all bearing some sort of fruit: grapes, potatoes, carrots, peaches, pears...you name it, and it was there. Above, a large animal which looked like a cross between a plant and a bird was singing in the trees. The creature was brown and covered in vines. She had a crown of leaves that was unique. For some reason, the crown of overlapping leaves was shaped like a dunce cap. Her horns were miniature trees. Instead of a normal tail, the end split into flowers.

"Hello!" Jade called out to the beautiful bird.

The bird turned. "Oh, hello, I didn't see you. Mistake me if I'm wrong, but aren't you the heir to the throne?" she chirped.

"Yes, what *are* you?" Jade replied.

"I am a *Platha*. It is Imaginese for plant-bird. The plural is *Plathai*. I am the daughter of the chief of the *Plathai*," she explained.

"Oh, that's cool…my name is Jade, by the way. What's yours?" Jade did not linger on any of what the bird had said.

"My name is Meadow. Hey, if you ever need a message-carrier or someone to talk to, I hang out here a lot because it's my designated area," Meadow squawked.

"Designated area?"

Meadow explained how each *Platha* gets his or her own area to study. They would study the animals that live there, the plants that grow there, and most important, finding out the balance in the area.

"This is the Croctail-Wollion Border Area. Sometimes, a couple *Platha* study in the same area together because of the space issue," Meadow tweeted. "Sadly, I got stuck with my jerk cousin, Creek."

"That stinks. Jerks are the opposite of perks, I always say. Hey, do you know a Wollion named Howler?" Jade asked.

Meadow smiled as much as a bird can smile. "Yeah, I'm practically his best friend. What about him? Do you think he's coming to kill you? He's perfectly nice."

"No, no, it's just that I'm meeting with him today and I was wondering if you knew him. Would you like to come?"

Meadow's smile faded. "I'd love to, but I have work. See you soon?"

"Of course! I really want to learn more about your species! And maybe you can help me learn to read Imaginese, even though the language sounds funny. Howler said that it's the language around here," replied Jade.

"Oh, Meadow!" Another plant-bird was calling for her. "Where aaaaaare youuuuu? Time for woooooorrrrk!"

"Ugh," Meadow sighed, completely disgusted. "That would be Creek. Oh, and just so you know, everyone in our

Platha Tribe hates Howler. But can you keep a secret? This information could help you."

Jade nodded. "What is it?"

"Oh, um, it's a cave. Only *Plathai* and royalty know about this, so I figured you should, too. Go to Tormakk Rock. Once you're in the tunnels, take two rights, a left, another right, go straight, and two lefts. Then take the straight path. Be careful; it's not mapped. Howler knows about it already—I have a big beak. Sorry, but I gotta fly!" Meadow turned and leapt off her branch and began to soar away.

"Wait!" Jade called. "What rock? Why is it helpful?"

But Meadow was already gone.

. . . . .

Jade looked at the clock. It was nearly ten o'clock and she kept thinking about Meadow's words: "Go to Tormakk Rock. Once you're in the tunnels, take two rights, a left, another right, go straight, and two lefts. Be careful; it's not mapped."

Great, she thought. *Only my first morning, and I already have mysterious directions to who-knows-where. I'm totally super-excited and not at all worried about this.*

Heavy paw steps sounded outside the hut. A *bang* echoed. Jade guessed he was trying to knock, as the voice of Howler asked, "May I come in?"

"Sure," Jade replied as she threw open the door.

"Hi, Meadow told me she told you I knew about the Tormakk Rock secret and she also told me we should go there!" Howler paused for a breath.

"Yes, well, it's been bugging me. Have you ever been to the place she was talking about? Apparently, it's a magic rock."

"Nah, I never had the time before, but it's in Wollion territory. You want to go?"

"A little adventure?"

"Yup."

"Before sunset?"

"Of course!"

"What should we bring?"

"Seriously? You're asking?"

"Nope, it's just a joke. We should bring water, food, a map, hiking boots, flashlights-"

"Okay, okay! I get it!" Howler said.

They packed some food, water, hiking gear, and crystal flashlights made from the automatic light system in the hut.

As they set out south to Tormakk Rock, Jade and Howler began to share their ideas of what was in the cave.

"Maybe it's the River of Healing mixed with the River of Strength!" Howler   suggested excitedly.

"Or maybe it's an infinite supply of food," replied Jade.

"Ooh, it could be some Words of Wisdom books!"

"It might be a secret passageway to Imagination Castle!"

Howler stopped suddenly in front of a large, gray rock. "We're here," he announced. "This is Tormakk Rock."

"Don't forget, take two rights, a left, another right, go straight, and two lefts!" Jade reminded him.

They reached the entrance to the cave and Jade flicked on the flashlights, as Howler couldn't turn on his flashlight while it was in his mouth. He led the way into the murky darkness, his spiky, furry mane spiked up as to warn off any man-eating, monster-headed, poison-spitting bad guys.

They reached the first crossroad. "Go right," murmured Jade. For some reason, she felt the urge to keep her voice down. Someone... some*thing* was watching them.

They followed Meadow's directions until they reached a big spruce door. Engraved on it, written in Imaginese, said:

"Choose right, you walk on.
Choose wrong, and you're surely gone.
Save a soul, and release a spirit,
or set a killer free,
and the bad spirit...you'll see."

Howler whimpered.

"Wow, cheery place. Thanks for translating." Jade shivered. It was quite cold. "I wonder why Meadow wanted us to come here."

"Well, do we enter?" Howler prompted. "I mean, if you want to come back tomorrow, or next month...or next year...."

"Howler, you big scaredy-cat, get over yourself!" Jade doubled over, laughing, because Howler looked so big and scary. It was hard to believe he was a big scaredy-cat.

"Hey! That is an insult to my kind!" Howler complained.

"Let's just get this over with already...and keep it down! I feel like we're being watched."

"Fine, fine," he replied, still muttering about how the phrase "scaredy-cat" was extremely insulting to anyone with feline blood.

Jade took a deep breath and pushed the large spruce doors open.

A large well stood in the center of the room. On one side, there was a circular, somewhat transparent cage with something inside. On the other side, same thing. But on the wall opposite the doors, was a long corridor dimly lit by torches. The well also had words in Imaginese. Jade asked Howler to read them out loud.

"If you reel in the bucket with the key,
Choose who you wish to free.
Or you could follow the passage dimly lit,
For what lays beyond, is a secret.
But be warned, release wrong one,

You're not going to have fun.
Choose the passage dimly lit,
You may consult the wrong spirit.
However, these are the tests,
And you will begin the long spirit quest."

"Meadow told me to take the straight path. What do you think we should do, Howler?" Jade asked.

"Straight is fine by me. Or, if you want to, we can come back later...," he muttered.

The doors slammed shut.

"Or not," she said.

"Straight, then!"

They went around the well and made their way through the dimly lit corridor. Looking to the side, Jade saw huge statues carved into the wall. They each had a crown that looked like a coiled Ridgeback Rattlesnake whose tail came out of its forehead. When the head of the serpent stretched around for the second time, its head came up into a threatening position. In the center of its head, though, was a diamond as blue as Howler's eyes. Ridgeback Rattlesnakes did not have diamonds in their foreheads.

Finally, they reached the end of the hall. This spread out into yet another circular room. But instead of a well, there was a large underground lake. There was a sky hole which let in a stream of sunlight.

Jade checked her new watch she had found in the hut. It said the time was almost 11:59. It beeped and changed to 12 noon. Suddenly, she began to hear something other than the gentle lapping of the underground lake.

"Do you hear...whispers?" Jade asked Howler. She hoped she wasn't hearing voices. After all, that would mean she either was already crazy, or she was slowly going insane.

"No," Howler scrunched up his face. "Am I supposed to?"

She wondered from where the voices were coming. But she received her answer when she walked in a kind of trance toward the lake, for the whispers grew louder.

As she peered into the weird silvery water, she saw something both creepy and amazing that she would never forget.

Ghosts.

Thousands swarmed under the surface of the lake, and all of them were trying to talk to her at once.

"Talk to me. I can give you all you've ever dreamed of," said one.

"Come here. I can lead you to a great destiny," said another.

"Release me."

"I'll give you power beyond your imagination."

"Help me."

"Howler, what is this?"

There was no answer.

Jade turned around. Howler wasn't moving. He was still standing in the same position. She waved a hand in front of his face...no reaction.

Howler was frozen.

Chapter Three:
Ghosts Give Bad Advice

If Jade had not felt like flipping out by the earlier scary writing, she definitely felt it coming on now. Her mind ran over the last few minutes: First, the creepy writing on the doors, second, the scary writing on the well, third, the ill-defined things in the circular cells, fourth, the hall of weird Ridgeback Rattlesnake crowns, fifth, the spooky ghosts and their voices, and now, sixth, Howler was frozen. She was torn between the idea of freaking out and listening to the ghosts.

She decided on listening.

The voices were just as weird and as ambitious as before, but they seemed to be fading and turning into much nicer voices. But it took a while.

"Talk to me. Together, we can take over the world!"

"Don't listen to that blob fish-faced piece of pygmy sperm whale poop! Talk to me."

"Here's a way to prove you are worthy for the throne: go jump off a cliff and live to tell about it."

"You and I are destined to work together."

"How about not listening to those scale-brains and talking to me?"

"With me, the Jews shall perish!"

Was that really Adolf Hitler?

"Talk to me, and we will end America! Great Britain will conquer all!"

King George the 3rd?

"Stop, stop, stop! Everybody, stop! She may only talk to ghosts without their own agendas!"

"Yes, we good ghosts outnumber you ten to one! After all, E=mc squared!"

Wait, was that Albert Einstein?

Jade had a feeling that by "she," they meant her. But that was okay, because good ghosts are better than bad ones. Eventually, the good ghosts had taken over the speaking in her head.

"Come, touch the Sacred Water of Great People."

"Yes!"

"Monkey gets told, monkey does! I would know, because I spent years and years of my life with them!"

Jane Goodall! Jade had loved learning about her. But she was still alive. What was *she* doing here? Maybe she had a special spot reserved for her. That didn't make any sense. Jade was in a world where mixed creatures roamed. What did "make sense" mean anymore?

"Just touch the water..."

The ghostly voices were impossible to resist. Jade leaned out and touched the water.

Instantly, she was sucked under. The darkness became darker as she shut her eyes. But the weird thing was, the water wasn't cold. Instead, was rather warm.

And then all of the darkness and water disappeared.

Jade opened her eyes. She was in a warm, sunny place full of flowers and creeks, lush forests and singing birds. In other words, it was Paradise.

"Welcome to the Important Spirit Afterlife," said a voice.

She turned.

There, in the clearing, stood a beautiful ghost. She had brown eyes, a shimmering white and gold dress, and long chestnut-colored hair. In other words, she looked like Jade.

"Uh, who *are* you?" Jade asked.

"I am Queen Stardust, more commonly known as the Best Queen. Just kidding! I'm actually not known as that," the ghost said. "I am known as your mother."

. . . . .

"I have missed so much of your life!" Jade's mother, Queen Stardust, exclaimed. "Tell me, what was it like in the mortal world?"

"Well," Jade said slowly, because this had been broken to her all at once, "I lived in a closet-sized room. It was surprisingly roomy because I didn't have anything except for a couple sets of clothes and a bed on the floor."

"Oh, so the *Hakuna Mawazos* kept you in one of those orphanages?"

"Yes, umm, what's a *Hakuna Mawazo*?"

"A *Hakuna Mawazo* is a person who has no imagination, therefore making it impossible for that person to get into the Kingdom of Imagination." Queen Stardust smiled at her daughter. "I'm afraid your father, King Moonstone, is busy at the moment. However, there are more important things.

"First of all, you have basically signed a contract saying that you will complete the long Spirit Quest. This means you go through many hard tasks in the Important Spirit Afterlife. But don't worry, if you die here, you just aren't allowed to touch the Sacred Water ever again, so you can't visit.

"Second of all, if you complete all three Trials, you must tell the Dragon of the Sun and Moon that you have completed the Spirit Quest.

"And lastly, you must free one of the spirits in order to leave. One is good, one is bad. My time with you is short. Please succeed the Spirit Quest so you can come back for cookies!" Queen Stardust's voice seemed to be growing fainter. Her body turned transparent.

"Mom! Wait, don't go, not yet! Where should I start?" Jade wailed to her mother.

But Queen Stardust was already gone.

At least she had the answer to her question.

Her star necklace heated up like it had fallen into a volcano and was melting. The world began to spin very fast; it was like going through a stormportal. But instead, she felt like she was being turned into liquid, and then gas.

The water cycle, Jade thought.

Then the world solidified. She fell flat on the ground. She picked herself up and promptly vomited on the grass.

"Jade Alexandra Skystone," said a voice, as if reading from a scroll. Jade hadn't heard her full name for a long time. "You have agreed to journey the Spirit Quest. This means you are set three hard tasks, or Trials, to find your place in the Kingdom. You will complete this by yourself. First task: Find your way through the Maze of Terror and reach the second task, which is a little bit harder."

Jade looked for the mystery voice. All she saw was a very depressing-looking stone maze. Actually, it was *scarier* than depressing. "Where are you? *Who* are you?"

The voice laughed. "You will see me at the end of the three Trials. But for now, focus on the Maze. I hope you live. I really want you to be able to come back. Just make it to the end. I will only be able to talk to you in between tasks. Rules: Don't die. Survive until you reach the end. No climbing over the walls! Be strong, because this is a test of strength. Ready, set, GO!"

Jade's body reacted without letting her think it through. She dove into the Maze, which instantly, she knew was very unwise.

Chapter Four:
Death and Monsters Everywhere

The entrance closed behind her. Instantly, terror swept through her body, taking all her confidence away. Panic seized her.

She ran; and ran; and ran, with no clue of where she was going. Twice she thought she saw the same creepy witch statue. But it wasn't until ten minutes later until something happened.

Something sticky surrounded her. She wriggled around, trying to get free. She felt the stuff tremble, then realized she was in the presence of a huge, furry shape with eight legs, a lot of eyes, a swollen rear end, and a foaming mouth with weird snappy things clicking together.

Jade was trapped in a giant spider web. Somehow, she knew a bug's number one rule when getting stuck in a spider web was *don't struggle*. That signaled to the spider something tasty was stuck in the web, trying to get free.

The oversized arachnid clicked its pincers menacingly. It looked extremely hungry.

"I will ask you a riddle. Answer it incorrectly, you die. Answer it correctly, you walk free. Choose not to answer, I leave you here to free yourself, which is impossible," he hissed. "Here is the riddle:

My gaze causes death
And so does my breath
You wouldn't make a sound
I live underground
I grow to be tiny
I hate weasels
What am I?"

Let's see, Jade thought, hoping she wouldn't get it wrong. This was just like the myth of Oedipus from Greek mythology, where he has to answer a riddle to get past the sphinx. *My gaze causes death, and so does my breath. You wouldn't make a sound. I live underground. I grow to be tiny. I hate weasels.* This sounded very familiar to Jade, but she couldn't quite put her finger on it. She was pretty sure the Dragon of the Sun and Moon had said something about the killing with look and the hatred of the weasels when they were walking to the Wild Croctails...

"Well,?" hissed the large arachnid. "What is your answer?"

"I-uh, I'm thinking." If the riddle said *my gaze causes death*, then could she find it and use it to get the giant spider looming over her to go away? But even if she found it, there was no chance it wouldn't breathe on her or kill her with a quick glance to the eyes.

Wait.

Airgor had said that basilisks wear special sunglasses to prevent people from getting killed! Was the basilisk the answer? Did it fit the riddle's description?

"Hurry up! I don't have all day!" he growled.

Okay, seriously. That spider needed a lesson on patience.

Time to see if basilisk was the right answer.

My gaze causes death. Check. A basilisk can kill with a single glance.

And so does my breath. Check. They have poisonous breath.

I live underground. Check. Basilisk venom kills everything around it so you can always tell where its hole is.

I grow to be tiny. Check. Basilisks can grow to be twelve fingers long, which isn't very long when you think about it.

"Are you done yet?" demanded the giant spider.

"Nearly," Jade replied.

I hate weasels. Check. Weasel stench is a basilisk's weakness.

"Is the answer a basilisk?" Jade asked. She bit her lip, sure she would get devoured any second now.

The arachnid paused. Then, "HOW DID YOU KNOW!" he shrieked.

"Airgor told me," she replied as calmly as she could, which wasn't very calm. On the inside, she was shaking with terror...on the outside, also shaking. It might have just been the Maze, though. However, she knew the spider could feel the sticky web trembling.

"Oh, he would know, all right!" yelled the arachnid angrily. "He simply *loooves* them, doesn't he? Because of him, EVERYONE knows the answer to my riddle!"

"Then try a new riddle. Meanwhile, we had an agreement; let me go," Jade responded. "Or do you want me to tell everyone who hasn't met Airgor the answer to your riddle and that spiders don't keep their promises?"

The spider paled as much as a black spider can pale. "Um, no, I guess we did have an agreement...and then if I didn't keep it I wouldn't get to eat...," he mumbled. "I guess I'll have to let you go."

The spider detangled the web from Jade. "Now, don't tell anyone the answer to my riddle," the arachnid said sternly. "And to tell the truth, I kind of like you. You're the first girl with a strong heart to come in centuries. The last one had a heart attack when she saw me. I didn't even get to ask my riddle!"

"Um, okay?"

"Now, skedaddle, or I'll catch you again! And just because I like you doesn't mean I won't eat you. I ate my favorite grandma!"

Jade ran as fast as she could in the other direction. Left, right, right, straight...it just got more confusing.

Then she stumbled into a stone clearing. In the center, a sword was stuck in the dirt. *Hmm,* that *could be useful,* she thought, and tugged the sword out of the ground.

A low growl echoed through the stone clearing. Red eyes bobbed in front of her. A hissing sound...then came a bleat like a goat in a pasture, and a disfigured outline.

Yellow, orange, and blue flames erupted in the darkness. Jade could now see the thing. Was it a Chimera?

With the head and body of a ferocious lion, the tail of a venomous snake, and a lawn-mowing goat head on its back, the Chimera was twice as frightening in the dark. The fact the lion head breathed flames didn't help.

At least she had a sword now.

Flames bursted out again from the lion's jaw, and Jade jumped out of the way, falling to the ground. The snake head lunged at her, so she rolled to one side. More flames. She rolled to the other side and came up kneeling.

The chimera charged! She readied her sword, hoping to impale it on its pointy side. The lion just breathed fire on her. Clothes smoking, Jade yelped and did the safety lesson she had learned at school: stop, drop, and roll.

She had to keep rolling around even after the fire was extinguished because the snake kept lunging at her in an attempt to strike. The goat bleated a lot and spit random bits of food at her. Jade had to be wary of flying projectiles.

The lion's paws slammed into her, pinning her to the ground. The sword was lying on the ground a few feet away. Jade stretched out her hand, trying to reach it. The snake hissed, about to strike the final blow.

Jade's hand reached the sword just as the snake struck. Somehow, she managed to react fast enough and slice off the snake's head.

The lion and the goat roared in anger and pain. A large paw scraped her arm, drawing a large amount of blood. The goat spat out more projectiles. The lion's tail, the snake's body, lay on the ground, limp.

Charging the Chimera-that-no-longer-had-one-of-its-heads, Jade started to think she could really win this fight, unless the chimera got more enraged and deadlier than a great white shark who just had his food stolen. Sure, it didn't have one of its heads anymore, but of course, that didn't mean it was defeated at all. On the contrary, *chopping off one head just made it more enraged and deadlier than a great white shark who just had his food stolen*. Whoops.

The lion head spewed more flames at her as soon as she rolled within range. The goat spit out a really large piece of something. She didn't want to know what it was. She needed to station herself behind the stupid creature and stick her sword into its butt. Fortunately, she found out at that moment that Chimeras are dumb.

Jade vaulted over the back of the Chimera, just behind the goat head. The lion breathed flames, but instead of hitting her, it hit the goat head in front of her.

You know what a goat on fire sounds like? It sounds like...a goat on fire. It shrieked in pain, as well did the lion. The flames spread onto the lion's back. It did exactly what Jade had done earlier, when her clothes had almost caught on fire. But it rolled onto a pile of dry leaves, and the leaves started to burn. Howling, the Chimera tried to escape, so Jade stabbed it. It roared once more before going still. The burning leaves became its grave.

She panted, trying to regain her breath. And then Jade ran for her life, for the sake of getting out of this horrid Maze. Just like the feeling of being watched in the caves of Tormakk Rock, she had a weird feeling that something was watching her.

She tried to gather information on what her senses told her: The smell of burning leaves behind her, the sound of wind through the vast Maze of Terror, the strange feeling of terror of the nine heads watching her….

Nine heads?

An acid-like scent burned the air. Jade knew about a creature in Greek mythology that had nine heads and smelled of acid. She had to get out...fast! And hopefully find the fire that sent the Chimera to its death, because only fire could defeat it.

The great nine-headed watching feeling just *had* to be a Hydra staring down at her, about to strike.

She ran fast, back the way she came. Back to the stone clearing where she had killed the terrifying Chimera.

The smell of burning leaves got stronger. But then, a blob of acid missed her by inches. The Hydra was at her heels.

Following the sound and smell of crackling fire, her senses told her she was near. Up ahead, she saw an orangish light reflecting on the tall stone walls.

Jade almost made it.

Two heads spat more acid directly in her path. She skidded to a halt. Looking left and right, she found there were no other paths. The only two paths were the acid-soaked floor in front of her, and the Hydra-guarded one behind her. She had to go somewhere. But where?

She decided to try and get to the fire. Backing up to get a running start, Jade leaped over the acid. The Hydra hissed in anger.

Her feet hit stone. She had made it! However, the Hydra was clambering over the acid. Jade looked wildly around for a stick.

There! Lying on the ground was a long, rough stick. She grabbed it and stuck the tip into the fire. She waited until the tip was on fire. Then, she rounded on the Hydra with the burning stick in one hand and her sword in the other.

Of course, only then did she realize the massiveness of the Hydra.

It spat more acid at her. She ducked. The Hydra swooped its head down to try and knock her over. That was the Hydra's big mistake.

Jade grabbed onto the head as it swung back up to join its others. It was quite easy, as the head had many humps and bumps on it. Once the head reached its height, she slid down it and chopped off the head at the base of the neck.

Eight of the heads howled. The ninth, which she had cut off, fell to the ground, dead. Jade quickly lit the bloody stump.

She tried the same tactic on the next head. Now, only seven heads howled, and two littered the ground. Sadly, the Hydra now knew her strategy. It bucked around, nearly throwing her off. Finally, it managed to get her off by using a head as a club.

Jade was knocked into the stone wall. A red haze filled her vision, and she thought she might have cracked a rib. The Hydra spit acid in her direction. She tried to get out of the way, but she was too slow. A droplet of acid landed on her arm. There was pain, so much pain, and she almost passed out.

The horrible feeling of acid filled her. Pain seared throughout her body. She could feel the acid burning through her skin, blackening the perimeter of the rough circle it had carved into her flesh. Howling, Jade tried to use her anger to give her strength, but it hardly worked. However, the pain made her want to smack the Hydra all the way to Erebos and back so she could do it again

She struggled to her feet, grabbing the sword and torch.

"YAAAGGGGHHHHH!" Jade yelled as she charged the Hydra again, trying to ignore the yellow spots dancing in her eyes.

The Hydra was so surprised, it recoiled. It looked at her as if to say, *How are you still alive, and how can you still fight...*which was probably the last thing the seven heads ever thought.

Everything went fuzzy. The only stuff Jade really remembered was a Hydra, a sword in motion, and a whole ton of screaming. Whether it was from pain or absolute madness, she didn't know.

Slice, burn, slice, burn—eventually all that was left of the Hydra was a bunch of diced Hydra pieces and a whole lot of blood. Maybe another monster would come along and have HydraBites for dinner rather than Roast Jade.

She looked up at the sky. How long had she been in the Maze of Terror? Thirty minutes? An hour? Either way, she had to get out. Besides, she had acid on her. Who knew how much longer she could last?

Jade struggled to her feet. Now, she could hear the faint whisper of a warm summer wind, and feel it blowing gently through the Maze. If she could follow it, maybe it would lead her out.

Leaning on the cold, smooth stone wall for support, she followed the slight breeze through the Maze.

She didn't see a single monster, which was really good. Maybe they were scared of the wind. Or, as she liked to think, they were scared of her.

The breeze picked up and got stronger. A bit of natural light began to seep in, wiping out the terror that had soaked into her body. Finally, she turned left and saw the exit. At last, a way out!

Jade started to hobble as fast as she could to the exit. Sunshine bathed her face, completely erasing all the terror within her. Even her acid-splashed shoulder felt better.

She had really done it.

She had really made it out.

Chapter Five:
Deck the Halls with Balls of Death

"Congratulations, Jade! Good job on not dying or going insane in the Maze of Terror! Nice sword!" The mystery voice rang out across the warm summer clearing. "I have this feeling you battled three monsters in the Maze just to see me."

"Okay, who are you?" Jade demanded. "And I most definitely did not walk through a giant, scary stone Maze of Terror and battle monsters just to see you!" she added.

"Never mind. So, you can survive the Maze, but can you survive the next Trial?" he said.

"Try me, Ghostman."

"The next Trial is...Deathball!"

"Say what, now?"

"Deathball is more than just giant flying balls of death. You must invade the ghost base successfully to pass the test. Use whatever you can. Good luck!"

Her necklace began to heat up again. The world folded around her, and she went through the water cycle once more. When everything solidified, she was standing in a wide-open field that had almost nothing but grass. About a hundred yards away, stood an old stone castle. Jade suspected this was the ghost castle she had to attack.

Step one: see what you can invade with.

She looked around. All she saw was a herd of Rhinolions. Maybe she could cause a stampede....

Step two: gather resources for invading.

"Hey, Rhinolions!" Jade yelled to the herd. Those within earshot looked up at her as she stood up on a nearby rock.

"Yes," they replied.

Jade nearly fell off her feet. Then she remembered she could speak to all of the creatures here. Duh!

"I need to talk to you all," she said.

As if on cue, ten of the Rhinolions ran off and told the others. Finally, the entire herd was gathered around her.

"Can you guys help me invade?" Jade asked.

"Of course we can," said a very large Rhinolion that the others seemed to follow. "That's why we're here."

"Are you the leader?"

He dipped his head. "Yes, I am Chief Loki, but my name doesn't mean I'm a trickster. This is my wife, Cleptora...." Chief Loki waved his tail to a beautiful Rhinolion. "And these are our cubs, Sabrina, Jake, Sandy, and Fang." Four tiny, adorable Rhinolions perked up at their names.

"So, would it be okay if any able-bodied Rhinolion helped?" Jade asked, feeling a bit awkward on the rock with everyone gazing up at her.

"Sounds fine. You are in charge."

"Okay," she called, her voice carrying across the plain. "Cubs, elders, sick Rhinolions...any of you not able to fight go stand over there." She pointed to her left. "The rest of you stay here and get ready."

"Spoken like a true leader," Chief Loki told her.

About a sixth of the herd went left and the rest stood on the right. As Jade hopped off the rock, she heard Fang and Sandy complain to their mother about not being allowed to go.

"But I can fight!" Sandy howled.

"I'm sure you can fight fine, but you're staying right here where I can see you," Cleptora replied sternly.

"We can take care of ourselves!" Fang added.

"No, you are going to stay right here."

Sabrina clotted Fang on the head as he tried to slip away while Cleptora helped Chief Loki with organizing the Rhinolions. "You heard her. She'd kill you if she found out went to fight!"

"Just because you're the firstborn doesn't mean you get to boss us around!" Fang argued.

"Yeah, who died and made you the Chief?" Sandy snapped right back at Sabrina.

"I'm going to sneak off anyway, no matter what Mom says!" bragged Fang.

"Guys, shut your snouts! Mom's coming!" Jake whispered frantically.

"Jade, honey, Loki needs to talk to you about the invading plans," Cleptora told Jade. "He's over there by the Rhinolions who are fighting, you see him?"

Jade squinted into the sun. "Yeah, I see him. Oh, by the way, I think Sandy and Fang are planning to sneak off and go fight."

Fang and Sandy did their best to look innocent.

Cleptora smiled exasperatedly, then turned around and immediately started scolding Sandy and Fang.

Jade walked over to Chief Loki and said, "I've never fought before, or commanded an army. Can you help?"

"This is your test, not mine. I've already passed," he replied. He must have seen the crestfallen look on her face because he added gruffly, "I suppose I could give you some pointers. I remember my first day as leader. I didn't know what to do."

She brightened immediately.

"First thing you need to do is get to know everyone, and get their opinion. You also need to know who you can and can't trust with power," Chief Loki began. "Then you should start thinking about battle plans, assigning duties, making generals...that kind of stuff. From there, it's easy. Get regular reports on everything going on around camp. Next is the battle. Fight, defend friends, defeat foes, and stay alive. Then you are a good leader," he finished. "Also, you cannot be respected until you have respected those in your charge."

"Wow," Jade said. "That sounds both easy and hard at the same time."

"You'll get the hang of it. But yes, it does take a while."

"I guess I'd better get started, then."

"Yeah, you probably should. I'd start to get to know that group over there by the very tall baobab tree, you see them? They're nice, and they always support their leader."

"Yes, I will. Thanks!" Jade jogged over to the small group of Rhinolions. There were only half a dozen.

"Hi," said the first Rhinolion. He was still young and had a tiny little strip of fur on his head for a mane. "I'm Apollo. What's your name?"

"I'm Jade," she replied. "What do you like to do?"

"I like to be with my best friends right here, under the shade of the baobab tree. Guys, say hello," Apollo said.

"Hello," said the other five in union.

A young female Rhinolion stepped forward. "I liked your speech a lot," she said softly. "I'm Meerkat." She certainly was small.

"And I'm Bull," added a large male Rhinolion.

"My name is Gray." His face was about as gray a Rhinolion could get.

"I am Pronghorn."

"Of course, Pronghorn goes before me, since he's the firstborn. Well, anyway, I'm Savannah, which is a much better name than yours, Pronghorn! Pronghorn antelope rely on savannahs to live!" said a female Rhinolion all in one breath.

"Pleased to meet you all," Jade told them. "I'd like to get to know you-"

"Jade!" Chief Loki called. "It is time to begin the fight!"

She ran over to him. "What happens first?"

"This!" He bounded up the large rock on which Jade had stood. "Rhinolions!" he roared, exposing many razor-sharp fangs Jade hoped to never have to face. "It is time to fight for the Castle of Ghosts again! Attack Formation Tiger!"

The crowd howled their approval.

If they are part lion, then why are they talking about tigers? Jade wondered.

The Rhinolions began to break up into groups of twenty, and the groups formed lines, two by ten. Then the lines became formations that made them look like tiger stripes.

Oh, so that's *why it's called Tiger Formation,* Jade thought.

The Rhinolions turned toward the ghost base. "Come on," Chief Loki said to her as he leaped off the rock. "They expect us to lead them!"

Jade drew her sword. Then, she and Chief Loki charged the ghost base, with thousands of Rhinolions behind them.

If you ever see an enraged rhino charging you, get out of the way fast. With the extra lion strength and roar, nothing is scarier than an angry Rhinolion charging at you. Also, bullfighting would not work on them.

When they reached the castle, arrows fell. Most Rhinolions had such thick hides that arrows only did minor damage, but others stumbled, an easy target. Their friends did their best to help get them moving.

The black gates opened, and ghosts poured out. A lot of large, bronze cannons rolled into view.

"Oh no," Jade murmured. "Not good, at all!"

The cannons fired.

Time slowed down. The metal balls sailed through the air. Then they landed.

The balls of death exploded. Rhinolions fell, consumed by the flames.

A ghost ran at her. She sidestepped and stuck out her blade. The ghost, who was running at top speed, found he no longer had a head.

Three more charged her. Jade could fight one, easy. Two, possible...but three? Doubtful!

Luckily, Bull saw her having trouble and came over to help. He was so big, he accidentally fell on one when another tried to stab him. But no doubt, it was useful.

As for Jade, she was more than happy to entertain the third. She sliced and jabbed at the ghost as if she had been training with a sword all her life. Blocking and parrying, she managed to avoid getting hurt.

But then the ghost faked a move and sliced open her left arm. Pain shot through her from fingertip to shoulder. It felt deep, but a lot of wounds were better than they actually looked.

Jade tried to perform the same trick on the stupid ghost. She pretended to jab at where the heart would be, and when the ghost blocked, she maneuvered her blade upward and stabbed the ghost in the face. The ghost dissolved.

"Thanks," she panted to Bull.

"No problem," he replied. "Friends help you kill bad dead guys." Then he raced off to help Savannah.

Jade spotted a squadron of ghosts terrorizing a couple of Rhinolions. She took off in their direction, sneaking up on a ghost and stabbing him in his spine. Talk about getting stabbed in the back.

The ghosts turned. The Rhinolions used this to their advantage. They leaped onto the remaining seven ghosts and started shredding them into piles of Chex Mix.

A ghost stabbed downward at her, and she only barely managed to parry the strike. Meerkat, who Jade had not realized was nearby, suddenly stood beside her and helped distract the ghost. Meerkat sliced her claws across his face, and the ghost disintegrated, screaming.

The pair made their way up a flight of stairs, slashing and slicing at every transparent enemy. The archers were still raining arrows, so Jade, Meerkat, and some other large, bulky Rhinolion that she didn't know, snuck up behind them and began killing all of the ghosts in sight. Well, re-killing, since they were already dead.

It went on like that for a while. Slashing, jabbing, and stabbing! Blocking and parrying! Re-killing ghosts! Occasionally saving a friend!

Finally, they made it to the top floor. Only about two dozen ghosts were left up here, for most were charging the enemy, getting torn to shreds, or disintegrating.

A big black flag with skull and crossbones on it waved in the wind. Lying in a heap beneath it was a white flag with a crown on it. However, five ghosts stood in their way.

"You're supposed to hang the flag," Meerkat told her. "Hunter and I will distract them, okay? For this battle to be over, you are the only one who can hang the flag."

"Okay," Jade replied.

"Ready, Hunter?" Meerkat asked.

"Of course," the big Rhinolion said confidently. "I was born ready!"

"Ready, set, go!" Meerkat said, and with that, she and Hunter charged the group of ghosts defending the flag.

Jade ran for the flag. When she got close, she dove under a ghost and reached for the white flag on the ground. Then, she hastily lowered the red flag, took it off, and hung up the white one. As Jade raised it to the top of the flagpole, Meerkat yelled, "Stop! We have won!"

The remaining ghosts slowly looked to the top of the flagpole. Their eyes widened as they saw the white flag with the crown on it flying in the wind.

A cheer rose up from the Rhinolions. They turned and faced Chief Loki, who was injured but alive.

"We have won this battle!" he roared to both Rhinolions and ghosts. "We will return home and spread word of our victory!"

The army of Rhinolions marched out of the Castle of Ghosts unchallenged. Jade, Meerkat, and Hunter made their way to the end of the victory marchers to join them. Whenever the Rhinolions passed one of their fallen warriors, they picked him or her up and carried them.

Finally, they made it back to the plains. Chief Loki made a speech about their bravery. The dead were placed in the center. Jade was sad to see among them Pronghorn, Gray, and one of the Rhinolions that had told the others of Jade's arrival.

When Chief Loki had finished talking, Jade thanked everyone for their help. As she hopped off the rock, Chief Loki pulled her aside.

"We will meet again," he said. "We mirror the Kingdom. We are here because we were called to battle the ghosts by you. I hope to share another battle with you soon. And don't worry, the dead will come back to life."

The world began to spin, and her necklace scorched her throat. She evaporated and reappeared in the same clearing as before.

"Welcome back!" said a cheerful voice.

Chapter Six:
How to Kill a Shadow
(Without Saying a Single *Star Wars* Quote)

Jade looked around, then remembered the speaker was invisible. "Well," she said, "let's get started already. I want to stop coming here, and I want to find out who you are. So, what's the next task? Night killing?"

Jade was only joking, but the voice replied, "You're not far off, actually. Though what is next is much harder than night killing. You're going to have to learn how to murder a shadow!"

"A shadow."

"Exactly!"

"Just one problem!"

"Yes?"

"You can't touch a shadow."

"I'm afraid you'll have to figure that one out on your own. Good luck!"

Her necklace burned once more. Jade evaporated again. At this point she was thinking, *Okay, really? What is it with the water cycle? Do they worship it?*

She precipitated standing next to a cave in a jungle. The cave was filled with hundreds of jades. They littered the floor, stuck to the walls, hung from the ceiling, and filled every nook and cranny.

A hissing noise filled the air. Slowly turning around, Jade saw a giant Burmese python slither out of a hole in the trunk of a thirty-foot-wide baobab tree. The python must have been at least forty feet long and wide enough to eat a car, which meant he was about three feet thick. His eyes were shut tight, as if the sun shone too brightly to look anywhere. She realized she no longer had a sword.

And then the snake spoke.

"Another one?" it rasped.

"W-what do y-you mean, another one?" Jade asked nervously.

"Another one for a training session!" The snake slithered a bit closer. Jade took an instinctive step back.

He hissed out some snaky laughter. "No need to be afraid. I helped them all, didn't I?"

"You 'helped them all?' Who did you help?"

"Why, the greatest kings and queens of the Kingdom, of course! How do you think your mother was initiated Queen?"

"Coronation?"

"No! She went through the Trials, and when she got to this one, I helped her."

"So, can you help me?"

"Once you properly introduce yourself."

"My name is Jade Skystone. What's yours?"

"My name is Upir. Now, let's get started, shall we?"

"Okay. Now, first off, don't freak."

Oh no, Jade thought.

And then he opened his eyes.

Jade freaked. The sight of what was underneath the eyelids made her shudder so bad she almost lost her breakfast, which was, surprisingly, still in her stomach.

Upir was blind.

It got worse. The poor guy wasn't just blind. Where his eyes should have been, there was nothing. Just a starry darkness!

"This is my curse," he said sadly. "But it is also my gift."

"Not to be rude or anything," Jade said, "but how is *that* a gift?"

"Because this allows me to see...not just in our current world, but everything. The past, present, and future of every world, except for my own."

"Well, then how is it a curse?"

"I only have one. No parents, siblings, or children. Because of my eyes, only one cares about me. Only Lady Anivia!"

"I'm sorry to hear about that. Growing up, I also only had one person. She's the headmistress of my old orphanage, Ms. Sanders."

"So we are on the same page, then?"

"Yes."

"Good...let's get started," Upir said. "So, if you're wondering why the cave is full of jades, it's because you can use them to create weapons. If you learn how to control this power, it should be strong enough to destroy the Darkness."

"And how exactly does that work?"

"Well, you take something that represents you, or your name, and use that connection to harness its power. Take the Dragon of the Sun and Moon, for example. Whether it was day or night, he could use that power to protect the Kingdom of Imagination. And if he was under the sky, he could sometimes gain so much strength that all of his spirals glow!"

"Wow."

"Go ahead and try concentrating on using the jades to create weapons."

"It's that easy?" Jade was thoroughly surprised.

"You wish. It takes lots of practice," he replied. "Try it anyway."

"Wait, isn't it 'Do or do not, there is no try'?"

"What?"

"It's one of Master Yoda's lines from *Star Wars Episode V: The Empire Strikes Back*. Have you ever seen it?"

"No, I don't watch movies. No eyes, remember? Now try!"

Jade walked toward the cave that she supposed was worth at least a million dollars. Under her breath, just for the kicks, she muttered, "'I am one with the Force, the Force is with me. I am one with the Force, the Force is with me.'"

"And please no more *Star Wars* quotes!" Upir called.

Once she was at the entrance to the cave, she began to imagine the jades melting together to form a sword.

"Concentrate! Remember to connect with the jades by using your name. Otherwise, it won't work. Use your emotions to help them know what you want them to form, got it?" Upir instructed.

"Got it," Jade replied.

She thought of herself as another one of the precious jewels, only she was the leader. She needed to protect her kingdom from evil. She needed to be strong, just like the jades. She needed to be able to fight with the ferocity of a Griffin defending treasure.

After what seemed like eternity in a conference with boredom and concentration, some of the jades shuddered and began to rise. Then, they came together and smelted themselves into a glowing green sword. It got so bright she had to look away. The glowing subsided, and Jade was left with a normal-looking sword, except it was still completely green.

"Cool! Magic sword!" she exclaimed.

"Good job!" Upir praised her.

"Thanks," she replied.

"Ready for the simulator?"

"Simulator? You didn't say anything about a simulator!"

He didn't respond immediately, but after about ten-seconds he said, "No, I suppose I didn't. Well, anyway, you're going to go through a simulator to test your skills against a replica of the Darkness. Oh, you might also want a shield."

Once she'd conjured a shield (which took much less time), Upir yelled, "Sword up, shield ready! Fight!"

He disappeared back into his hole in the baobab tree.

An inky black darkness, blacker than a midnight with no stars and no moon, had begun to creep out of the forest shadows.

Jade raised her sword and shield. Just in time, too.

The bit of Darkness lunged at her. She sliced at it, but missed. The Darkness knew she was unbalanced and gave her a little nudge. Jade almost toppled over.

She slashed at it again, and this time the sword connected, though that time it seemed like the magic sword helped her out. But either way, a hit was a hit.

The darkness wailed: a long, horrible, screeching sound that came from the direction of the darkness.

Jade stabbed downward at the darkness. Her previous sword-fighting skills helped guide her hand to what should be a heart.

Screaming louder, the darkness began to evaporate— the holes Jade had made were eating into its ghostly form. Soon, it was gone.

Upir slithered out of his hole again. "Good job," he said. "But now let's make it a bit harder, shall we? Prepare for level two. Shield up, sword ready! Fight!"

He slithered back into his hide-y-hole.

Couldn't you give me a bit more of a warning before you head back into your treehouse? Jade wondered.

This time, the Darkness came from all around her. It closed in, shrinking her space. Jade knew if she hesitated, she would die. So, she did the natural thing: she swung the sword.

The darkness leaped back to avoid being hit. Then it attacked from behind. As soon as about a cubic foot of the

Darkness touched her, she began to lose feeling wherever it touched, and begn to suffocate. Whirling around, she slashed as far as she could into the Darkness that was suffocating her.

It screamed so loud Jade's ear drums almost popped. But after a moment, the hole began to smoke, and then it began to close. After about ten-seconds, it was completely closed.

Hmm! More mass, faster healing? Jade thought.

She raised her green shield, which was also guiding her hand, to fend off another attack. She struck again, burying the sword in so deep her hand almost touched the Darkness. More howling! Pulling her sword out, she slashed at another bit of Darkness. She repeated the attack, creating two wounds for every one that closed. Wails filled the air, and Jade almost became deaf.

Eventually, the Darkness evaporated. It was all shadows of the sun now.

Upir slithered back out of his hole. "Well," he said dryly, "I guess I taught you well."

"Thanks, Upir! You helped me learn so much!" Jade replied. "By the way, does this kind of magic have a name?"

"Yes, it is called Lunar Twilight Magic. But this trial is far from over. You still have much to learn."

"Wait, what?"

He hissed a laugh. "Just messing with you! Sheesh, can't a lonely old snake with no eyes and sees the past, present and future of every world except for his own have a sense of humor?"

"Of course you can!" Jade said indignantly. "But please not *that* joke. I'm done with these trials!"

"Okay, okay! Just come and visit me at Imagination Castle," Upir said.

"You live at Imagination Castle?"

"Yes, the baobab tree is in my room."

"How does a baobab tree that size fit? You know what? Never mind. Forget I said anything."

"Oh, they're calling for you in... Three, two, one! Bye!" Upir waved his giant speckled brown tail in her direction.

Of course, the star necklace scorched her. And then Jade evaporated. Again!

. . . . .

"Look who's back!" the mystery voice exclaimed.

"Show yourself!" Jade demanded. "I completed the trials."

"All right, keep your head on. Ready to see who I am?"

"What do you think? Of course! I've been bugging you about this since I first heard your annoying voice!"

Mist collected together, forming a human shape. A man roughly six foot five appeared. He spread his arms wide, as if inviting her in for a hug. Then he said, "Daddy's home!"

Chapter Seven:
The One on the Right is on the Left

"Wait, you're my dad and you didn't tell me for THREE DRAGON DUNG TRIALS!" Jade shouted. Then she raced in for a hug.

He gave her a pained smile. "Sorry, little gem, but your mother made me. I wish I didn't have to, but rules are rules. Especially when someone like your mother made them. She scares me."

"Really?"

"You bet. If you'd ever seen your mom on the battlefield, you'd be terrified, too. She's the scariest woman ever."

"I missed you and Mom so much," whispered Jade. "Hold on! If you're a ghost, then why can I touch you?"

King Moonstone sighed. "I wish I could answer that question, but alas, I still haven't figured it out. It's so confusing."

"Well, maybe you are solid when you want to be and vice versa."

"That *does* make a lot of sense."

"I know. I'm smart!"

He laughed, but then his smile faded. He tilted his head as if he heard something. "Sorry, little gem. You're about to exit the Sacred Waters of Great People. Come and visit soon, though!"

"I'm *leaving*? But I don't want to leave!"

"Don't forget about the cages in that main room," he reminded her. "You still have to choose a prisoner to free."

"Let me guess. You can't tell me which one I should free."

"Bingo."

"I'll visit. I promise!"

"You'd better!"

The world began to dissolve.

"I love you, Dad," Jade said.

The last words she heard her father saying on her first time meeting him were, "I love you too, little gem."

.   .   .   .   .

"Do you still hear voices?" Howler's voice filled the cave.

"Howler!" Jade raced over to his side and gave her friend a fierce hug.

"Watch the mane! I groomed it this morning!" he complained. "Seriously, what got you so ramped up?"

"Long version or short version?"

"Is there a medium version?"

"No."

"I guess short version, then."

"Okay. Voices. You froze. Mom! Mystery man! Trials! Maze! Giant spider! Chimera! Hydra! Mystery man! Deathball! Rhinolions! Ghosts! Capture the Flag. Mystery man! Upir! Cool magic green glowing sword and shield. Darkness level one! Darkness level two! Mystery man is Dad!"

"You know what? I change my mind. Long version."

"Good choice!" And so Jade started to tell Howler the entire story. She had only gotten to her encounter with the Chimera when they entered the room with the cages.

She walked toward the old stone well and began to reel up the bucket. Once it was at the top, she reached into the wooden bucket and pulled out an old, rusty gold key. On its side, there were words engraved in Imaginese.

"Howler, could you read what it says?" Jade asked.

"You only had to ask," he replied. "Let's see… The one you want and wish to free is on the right…or the left, you see."

"That makes absolutely no sense. But it reminds me of this awesome Johnny Cash song, *The One on the Right is on the Left-*"

"Jade."

"Oh, right, sorry!"

Jade looked left at the container. Something very black was oozing around inside of it. "Not that one," she decided.

Howler looked right. "I wish not this one either, but it looks like we have to."

"What do you mean?"

"Look." He pointed a large paw at something silver hovering in the back of the cage. It was a large key that looked like it fit the lock on the doors.

"I don't like the feeling in my gut that this is a really, *really* bad idea."

"Ditto."

Jade walked toward the cage, key in her hand. She put it in the lock. Taking a deep breath, she twisted the key.

The cage door creaked open. The thing inside it hissed like a leaky balloon. It floated out of the cage, its void-black substance whirling.

"Oh, no! No, no, no… This *cannot* be happening!" Howler whimpered.

"What is that thing?" Jade said nervously.

"*It!* We just released the Darkness. This is the thing that killed your parents."

"*What*? Oh, it did, did it?" she growled.

The Darkness spoke. *"Your parents were weaklings. You are a weakling too. I will destroy you and your puny friend,"* it hissed.

"Not on my watch," she hissed back. "Howler, get the key!"

He nodded and leaped around the Darkness. Sprinting toward the cage with his back turned on the Darkness, he didn't realize it was about to strike.

"Howler, look out!" Jade shouted.

He twisted out of the attack, but the Darkness was still fixed on him.

She had to act fast. She realized, that since they were underground, there were probably thousands of jades. She expanded her senses, calling out for the precious gems. Upir had told her to use her emotions. Well, she wanted to stick a magic sword right into the Darkness' butt, wherever it was. So, she used that emotion to create weapons to do it with. The cave rumbled. Suddenly, glowing jades appeared. They smelted themselves into a sword and shield.

The Darkness was still attacking Howler. Hardly thinking, Jade hurled her sword right into where the neck should be. The Darkness screamed and wailed. This gave Howler a chance to grab the key. Racing back to her, he dropped the key into her hand. She pushed it into the lock on the doors and turned it. The doors swung open. They bolted out.

"Go, go!" Howler yelled.

"Two rights, go strait, a left, another right, and two lefts!" Jade yelled back.

"How do you know?"

"I reversed the directions Meadow gave us!"

They reached the first crossroad. Howler bolted right. By the time they got to the next turn, Jade was in the lead. But at the next crossroad, when Howler was ahead, he hesitated.

"Straight, left, right, and two lefts!" she panted.

The Darkness was on their tail. After taking the last correct turns, with much needed reminders from Jade, they burst out into the blinding sunlight. The Darkness popped out of the cave and disappeared.

"What just happened?" she asked.

Howler looked very relieved that the Darkness had disappeared. "Security! My aunt, Juno, told me about the war, and that Lady Anivia had installed some, ah, *safety features* to the Kingdom. That particular one could also be used to create a mass evacuation if the Kingdom got in trouble. It would transport the entire population to another Kingdom."

"Whoa."

"I know, right?"

A shadow fell across them, as Airgor landed in front of them. "Well," he growled. "Here are my two little adventurers."

Jade and Howler stayed silent.

The Dragon of the Sun and Moon threw back his head and laughed. "Just kidding! You should see the looks on your faces! Priceless! Just try not to get yourselves killed, okay? How would I explain it to your mother if you suddenly appeared in the Important People Afterlife? Dang, that woman *scares* me!"

"Queen Stardust," Howler said, "scares *you*."

"Imagine Fenris Wolf from Norse mythology. Now imagine him a thousand times scarier, riding a glowing horse, wielding a shiny sword and shield, and screaming bloody murder at everybody," Airgor said dryly. "That's Queen Stardust!"

"Hang on. How did you know we were going to be here?" Jade asked.

"Who did you think told Meadow to sit outside your hut and tip you off about Tormakk Rock's royal secret?" he replied.

"You made this happen?" Jade asked incredulously. "You almost got me killed about eleven times!"

"Sorry, but technically, you almost got *yourself* killed eleven times," he answered.

Jade couldn't help smiling a bit at that. After all, what she had just been through was scarier than any childhood bully. It had cracked her "crazy shell" a little.

"Although I did forget you had to open one of the cages to get out," the Dragon of the Sun and Moon frowned.

"You had to remind us about that now," Howler said, "when we just got out of there."

He shrugged. "Eh! You'll have to face worse eventually."

"Because the Darkness was released?" Jade said.

"Yes, we just have to cross our talons and hope he doesn't attack anytime soon. Oh, I must go tell the Wild Croctails if you completed the Trials. Did you?"

"I did. In fact, I have to finish telling Howler what happened down there."

"Well, hurry up, because when I get back, you have to tell me what happened. Go back to the hut when you two are finished talking, okay?" Airgor spread his massive wings and launched himself into the midday sky.

"So," Howler prompted, "The Chimera!"

Jade continued to tell him about her adventure in the Important Spirit Afterlife. Howler kept saying, "Wow!" or "Scary," or "What happened next?"

When she was finished, Howler looked up at the sun. Her watch beeped. Looking down at it, she saw it was 1:00 already.

"I have to get back to my Prack. There's a missing Wollion, Hora," Howler said. He seemed extremely worried.

"Prack?"

"Short for Pride-Pack. It's a Wollion thing."

"I can tell. See you later!"

Howler turned and bounded into the dense forest.

Jade took out the map Hooktail had given her—which she would never leave in the hut, because she usually got lost in new and confusing places—and opened it up. She looked for Tormakk Rock, which was in the Southwest corner of Wollion territory. The hut was in the Northeast corner of the territory.

Well, Jade thought, *Howler ran off over that way, which means that's the village.* There was a dot on the map labeled *Wollion Village.* She wouldn't be able to pass by even the very edge of the main village if she were to make the quickest time.

She began to walk. By the time she got back, Airgor was already there, sitting outside the hut, for he most definitely could *not* fit in the hut.

"Spill," he said.

So she repeated the story for him. It was kind of boring, saying it over again, but he was more patient than Howler, who interrupted her every four-seconds.

Even after she finished, he was still silent. But then he said, "Your coronation will be on Friday at Starfall."

"Starfall?"

"Dawn. It's also known as Sunrise and Moonfall. Dusk is Sunfall, Moonrise, and Star-rise. Midday is Middlesun and Highsun. Midnight is Highmoon, Highstar, Middlemoon, and Allstars."

"Oh."

"Don't forget any of those, or the date for the coronation. It's only three days from now. Get something nice to wear. Here's some money! For the record, the Creatures of Mixed Life territory has great products."

Out of a scaly pocket in his side, which seemed to actually be a *part* of him, he took out a small, brown leather sack that jingled. "Gold-Silvers are coins. As the national currency, they're accepted anywhere." He handed her the sack.

"Thanks," Jade told him.

"You're welcome. I've got to tell the entire Kingdom that your coronation is on Friday." The great big dragon spread his gold and silver wings and soared away in the light breeze.

Since she didn't want to go many places alone, she thought about what Chief Loki had said: Get to know your people. So, she would go make a friend.

As she left the hut to go to the Creatures of Mixed Life territory, something rustled behind her. Whipping around, she saw that weird dragon-like creature with the double snouts, three eyes, a unicorn horn, a devil tail, and no wings.

Realizing he'd been caught, he hopped out of the bushes.

"Sorry, Princess Jade," he said sheepishly. "It *is* Jade, right? But I was in the Croctail village when the Dragon of the Sun and Moon told us of your success. So, like any curious Bi-mouth Tri-ocular Dragicorn, I followed you on my way back." He used both of his snouts to talk, so it sounded like two voices.

"It's fine. I just have three questions. One: What's your name?"

"Oh, well, my mom had a bizarre list of names for me and my siblings, and I got to be Illuminati because of...you know...three eyes." Illuminati said.

"Two: Why were you in the Croctail Village?"

"I have a dragonet-sitting job there. My dad's childhood Croctail friend, Illistria, has five dragonets: Sugarbite, Diamond, Demon, Sharptooth, and Solphoenix. They're a clawful. But at least I get five Gold-Silvers per day!" He brightened at the thought.

"Three: What exactly did you call yourself again?"

"A Bi-Mouth Tri-Ocular Dragicorn! It's just Dragicorn for short."

"Well, that's a mouthful. No pun intended."

"I know, right?"

"Can you help me find some good shops to buy things for the coronation? Considering you live in the Creatures of Mixed Life territory, I thought I'd ask you."

Illuminati brightened immediately. "Of course!" he said. "Let's go shopping!"

Chapter Eight:
Shopping with Three-Eyed Unicorn Dragons

While they walked, Jade pumped Illuminati with questions. She asked about his family, his home, and all the creatures of the Kingdom of Imagination.

"What's your family like?" she said.

"I live with my parents, a brother, and two sisters. My brother is the oldest. His name is Hades, because of the tail. But my twin sisters are the real she-devils. Their names are Tana and Teena. They're the youngest," he replied.

"Where do you live?"

"It's a small town called Hada. There, everyone knows everyone some way or another. I live near the Yhulriver Library."

"How many different types of creatures are there in the Kingdom of Imagination?"

"Unknown."

"What types of creatures do you know?"

"Too many to count."

"Well, just tell me the ones you know, then."

"Are you sure you want me to do that?"

"Positive."

"I guess I'll start with the Supreme General of All Armies," he began. "She's a Flame-Eye Bird's Wing, and she's the only one of her kind. Her name is Caralin."

"What does she look like?"

"Human body, horns, eagle wings, a beak, super spikey tail, eagle feet, flaming eyes, and talons instead of fingers. When she comes across an enemy, she sucks out their soul. They die instantly."

Jade immediately knew that General Caralin was no Flame-Eye Bird's-Wing to mess with. Anyone who could suck out a soul was someone to watch out for.

"Now on to the creatures near where I live," Illuminati continued. "Let's see...I guess I'll point them out as we go. Oh, look! There's a Banded Lemur Bird in the trees, you see?"

The Banded Lemur Bird had a very long, thick tail that looked useful for climbing trees. The beaked animal had a black "band" around his neck, which was actually made of fur, not an actual band. He also had clawed feet that would be good for leaping from tree to tree.

"That's Monkey," he said. "Hi, Monkey!"

Monkey looked down and waved.

They passed a creature that had a lion's head and body (mostly). Instead of a mane, the creature had a small goatee. The tail was a king cobra.

"What's that creature?" Jade pointed to the animal.

"That's a Horned Lionsnake," he replied. "Only the males have goatees. Look up."

She did.

Stretched above them, all seven colors shining clearly, was a shimmering rainbow. But above the first one sat another one. The thing about the second one, though, was the colors were reversed.

"A double rainbow," Illuminati said. "That is really rare. Look how happy the Rainbow Dragons are!"

Dozens of brightly colored dragons were swooping and soaring around the rainbows. Some treated the double rainbow as a slide. Happily skidding down it, they sent showers of multicolored sparks to the ground.

Continuing to walk, they came across another strange creature.

"That's a Brontodragon! Don't talk about the wings. It's rude. And I'm pretty sure that the wings are magical," he explained.

A very small brontosaurus was tromping through the meadow. She yawned, exposing dragonish teeth. Miniscule dragon wings on her back was what made her weird. All of a sudden, she stretched her little wings out and took off. Illuminati had been right, Brontodragon wings were magic.

They walked on. Jade almost stepped on a little winged mouse with hooves instead of hind paws. His stinger dripped poison.

"Sorry!" she apologized to the little guy.

He bared his tiny little fangs in a smiling way. "It's fine," he replied. "Happens all the time. Hey, aren't you my dad's weed control guy?" he asked Illuminati.

"The Denzil house?"

"Yeah...Oh, here's your payday! We forgot to leave it under the bush this time. Sorry! Here it is."

The rodent handed him a little bag tied with string.

"Thanks, Dougal."

"No problem!" he squeaked, racing off.

"What creature is Dougal?" she asked.

"He's a Demon Mouse...cute but deadly."

"Deadly? He doesn't look deadly."

"Looks can be deceiving."

As they headed towards Hada, they reached a cliff overlooking the town. In the center of it stood a large, golden statue of a giant winged king cobra with a feathery Mohawk. Its beak looked really sharp.

"That's the statue of Hada the Giant Woodpecker Snake—he's the founder of the city," Illuminati said. "Let's head down the trail."

Jade noticed a narrow path leading down the cliff. It wound down to a river, over which a bridge spanned it from bank to bank.

When they made it down the rocky trail, over the bridge, and past the sign that read WELCOME TO HADA, they could see everything much better.

There were grocery stores, funhouses, diners...they all had names like Thunderbird Gaming, Shika Grocery, and Luna Road. What they didn't see, though, were many clothing stores.

"We only use clothes for formal occasions," Illuminati explained, "such as weddings or coronations. There's only one shop for clothes here, but it's the best in the whole territory."

They turned a corner. In between the entrance to Lightning Neighborhood and Dalar Park sat a small clothing store. The sign above it read: SANDYPOOL'S CLOTHING STORE—ALL CLAW MADE.

"What creature is that running the store?" Jade asked him.

"That's Sandypool...she's an Oasis Bird."

A very large four-legged bird with the same tree horns as Meadow was running the shop. It was the same type of bird Jade had seen on her way to meet the Wild Croctail Dragons. Her body looked exactly like an oasis.

They opened the door and stepped inside. Sandypool looked up.

"Oh, hi Illuminati, " she said. "Aren't you going to be the new Queen?" she asked Jade.

"Yes," Jade replied.

"We don't get many human visitors here, but I'm sure I can find something for the coronation. Come on, let's find something pretty to match that necklace," she said.

Jade followed Sandypool into the back room. It was filled with thousands of fancy clothes. Sandypool led her over

to the Human section. There were dresses, tuxedos, suits...
literally every nice outfit Miranda Kerr could imagine.

"Five feet two inches tall, dress size 14-16?" Sandypool
estimated.

"How do you know my exact size?" Jade demanded.

She shrugged. "It just pops into my head."

"That is really useful for a seamstress."

Sandypool went over to a rack with lots of puffy
dresses. She rummaged around for a bit, then pulled out a
long, green dress with flowers decorating the hem. It was very
sparkly.

"Hmm, this ought to fit," Sandypool said. "Go try it on.
The dressing room is over there." She pointed a claw over to a
door on the left.

As soon as Jade walked out of the dressing room,
Sandypool exclaimed, "You are simply gorgeous! It fits you so
well! Give it a twirl."

She obeyed.

"I love it!" Sandypool said.

"I love it, too," Jade replied. "How much does it cost?"

"Oh, only thirty Gold-Silvers and a shout out to my
store, and that's quite a bargain for a dress as beautiful as this
one! One of my finest creations," she added proudly.

Jade changed back into her old clothes and took the
sack of coins out of her pocket. She counted out thirty Gold-
Silvers and handed them to Sandypool.

"Pleasure doing business with you," Sandypool thanked
her. "And don't forget about the shout out!"

"Don't worry, I won't," Jade replied. "Out of ten, your
service was a hundred."

Sandypool beamed.

As Jade and Illuminati exited Sandypool's Clothing
Store, they found another shop that was called SAPPHIRE
SHOES.

"You *need* to get some nice shoes," Illuminati said. "There is no *way* you are going to become Queen in your sneakers."

After doing some more shopping (and getting a pair of high heels studded with diamonds), the pair realized it was almost Sunfall.

"Dinner?" Jade asked.

"Sure," Illuminati replied.

They decided to go to Fire Boar Diner. It was a large place with many different types of amazing creatures.

Their waiter was a creature that looked like a cat with a shell on his back. He said, " I am Udolf, and I will be your waiter for this evening. Can I get you something to drink?"

"Water, please," Illuminati said.

"Do you have Hi-C?" Jade asked.

"We don't have that," Udolf replied. "But we do have a very nice fruit drink."

"Then I'll have some of that," Jade decided.

When Udolf left to get the drinks, Illuminati told her about the waiter. "He's a Snag," he explained, "a snail-cat."

They ordered dinner when Udolf returned with drinks. Jade got a Caesar salad. Illuminati got the soup of the day.

Their dinner got there in about twenty-five minutes. Illuminati's tomato soup had olives in it. Jade's Caesar salad was delicious. By the time they left, it was in between Sunfall and Allstars.

"Thanks for dinner," Illuminati said. "See you soon? I'm babysitting again tomorrow. Maybe you could drop by and help."

"Sure," Jade replied. "What a fun and horrifying day! Hard to believe that only this morning I was running from shadows."

He laughed. "Maybe you could drop by around 2:00. After nap time is when they're rowdiest, and then you can tell me how you were running from the dark. See you around." He yawned widely, his two snouts opening and closing.

They parted ways. A shadow fell on Jade. Looking up, she saw a small, silver dragon with a crescent moon on her head and tail swooping around the moon. Her little moon horn matched the phase exactly. Maybe they were connected somehow.

When she got back to the hut, Jade's head immediately hit the pillow. But as soon as she fell asleep, she had a horrible nerve-racking nightmare.

Chapter Nine:
Babysitting is Worse Than Fighting the Darkness

She started out in a dark, spooky cave. The Darkness swirled around. An indistinct figure was kneeling before the darkness. The thing seemed to be talking, but she couldn't make out the words.

Then the Darkness hissed in its awful voice, "Very well. Begin the process."

A chamber appeared. Inside it was a raging Wollion.

"Let me go!" she roared angrily. "The Kingdom of Imagination will have your life taken for this crime!"

"Patience, Hora," the Darkness said. "You will be useful to me soon."

Hora! This must be the missing Wollion Howler was talking about.

The indistinct figure pulled a lever. Darkness filled the chamber. Whether it was *the* Darkness or something else, Jade didn't know.

The Wollion, Hora, howled in pain. Jade wished she could do something, but it was only a dream. The darkness filled Hora. She writhed and thrashed. Soon, it was so dark she could no longer see the poor Wollion. When the darkness emptied, there was no more good creature of the Kingdom of Imagination. All that was left of her was a black shape that resembled her. She had pure white eyes with no pupils. All that was left of her was evil.

"Success," the Darkness said, satisfied. "Gredra, you have created a formula to change good to evil. I am pleased."

"Thank you, King," Gredra replied. "I would do anything to help you."

The Darkness addressed Hora. "Who do you serve?" he asked.

"The Darkness," she answered in a husky voice. "I serve the Darkness."

. . . . .

The next day at 1:30, Jade left the hut to help Illuminati babysit the Wild Croctail dragonets. She looked down at the map and willed it to zoom in so the hut was in one corner and the Croctail Village was in the other. Then she began to follow the path.

When she arrived, the dragonets were waking up.

"Thank Anivia," Illuminati said. "Perfect timing."

A big Wild Croctail Dragon lumbered up. "Illuminati told me you were coming today," he said. "Hopefully you'll be able to distract them from climbing all over me! I'm Spitvenom, these crazy little guys' grandpa. How are you doing?" Spitvenom held out his claw.

Jade shook it. "I'm doing fine." *Except for that dream last night.* "How are you?"

"Okay," he replied. "A few creaky bones here and there, but what do you expect when you're two hundred years old?"

"Two *hundred*?"

"Most dragons go up to two hundred ten."

"Hi, Grandpa!" A little over hyper dragonet gave Spitvenom a hug.

Illuminati said, "That's Sugarbite. Over there is Demon, Solphoenix, Sharptooth, and Diamond." He pointed them out. "Sugarbite is the youngest, then Demon, then Diamond, then Solpheonix, and then Sharptooth."

Sharptooth bounded over. "Hello!" he said to Jade. "What's your name?"

"I'm Jade," she replied. "I'm going to be your new Queen."

"Oh, I remember who you are! I think Demon's in love with you."

"Am not!" Demon exclaimed.

"Stop arguing!" Illuminati interrupted. "You should know better than to argue."

All of a sudden, Diamond and Solphoenix pounced on Sharptooth and Demon. They were so busy arguing, they didn't realize Diamond and Solphoenix were planning an attack.

Sugarbite saw the action and bounced over, whacking no one in particular with her tail.

"Whose side are you on?" Diamond demanded.

"No one's!" Sugarbite said, happily clubbing Demon over the head.

Jade was about to stop the fight, but Illuminati stopped her.

"Don't," he warned. "Fighting is good for them. This will help them sharpen their fighting skills for when they're defending the Kingdom."

Solphoenix pinned down Demon, and Sharptooth got Diamond. Sugarbite was still choosing no sides and hit everyone.

The four older ones got up and looked at each other. Jade knew what they were thinking.

"Four against one," Solphoenix said.

The others nodded in agreement. Then they all attacked Sugarbite. She was buried under a mass of small, wiggling green limbs.

Then the four attackers were blasted back in a radioactive light. Sugarbite was glowing pine green, the color of her scales. A bright green thing that looked like the Eye of Horus was around both of her eyes.

Jade had no idea what was going on. When Demon, Diamond, Solphoenix, and Sharptooth got to their feet, they stared at their little sister. The glowing died down.

Solphoenix said, "You freak. You don't belong here!"

"Solphoenix!" Illuminati scolded. "Take it back right now! Sugarbite is your sister!"

The whole Croctail Tribe was watching, but only Jade noticed that Sugarbite had slunk into the forest. She raced after the little dragon.

When she caught up to her, she was hopping from branch to branch, trying to get to the top of a tall tree.

"Sugarbite," Jade called.

She looked down at her. "Go away," she sniffled. "No one likes me. Why bother pretending?"

"I do like you," Jade replied. "And I have a friend who has a similar problem."

"There's someone like me?" Sugarbite asked curiously.

"Well, not *exactly* like you. He's a giant Burmese Python. His name is Upir, and no one likes him, either. He has a gift, too."

"Really?"

"Yes, and only Anivia cares about him."

"What's his gift?"

Jade thought for a moment, trying to figure out how to say it without mentioning his eyes. "He can see the past, present, and future of every world, except for his own."

"Wow. Why don't people like him?"

"Can I avoid this question?"

"Please?" Sugarbite put on such a cute face, Jade could hardly resist.

"Can you handle extremely gross stuff?"

"Of course I can!" she insisted. "I have three older brothers and an older sister who shows me whatever she's chewing!"

"Okay," Jade decided, "but this is really unimaginable. Don't tell anyone. Promise?"

"Promise."

She sighed. She had been hoping that Sugarbite would back out. *Time for the second plan,* Jade thought. "He's blind."

"Why is that so bad?"

"Are you absolutely positive you can handle this disgusting bit of news?" she checked. "Not backing out, or anything?"

"Never," Sugarbite replied.

Jade took a deep breath. "Upir isn't just blind," she explained. "He doesn't have any eyes."

"That's so horrible!" she squeaked. "That is totally making my *What Was Anivia Thinking* list!"

"My guess is that every gift comes with curse," she answered. "Otherwise there wouldn't be a balance."

"That makes some sense, I guess," Sugarbite said. "And if Anivia made one person special without a curse, then everyone would complain it wasn't fair."

"True. So consider yourself lucky."

"Why am I lucky?"

"Because you have a gift."

"Oh! Can I meet Upir?"

Jade remembered she had promised to visit the old snake in his baobab tree. "Maybe," she decided.

"Okay!" Sugarbite said happily. "Do you want to do something fun together? At least until my mom gets back?"

"Sure," she replied. "I remember when I was tortured by older kids. They used to pull this really mean trick where they put shaving cream on your hand and then tickled your face with a feather while you were sleeping. The person would reach up and rub their face and get shaving cream everywhere."

Sugarbite giggled. "Did that ever happen to you?"

"Loads of times. It was really annoying. But one time, I got together some allies and returned the trick to every kid who did it."

Sugarbite wrapped her tail around the branch where she was sitting and dropped down. Swinging back and forth, she asked, "Are you going to be like Solphoenix and the others, or are you going to be nice forever?"

"Don't worry, I'll be nice forever," Jade assured her. "Why wouldn't I be?"

"I don't know," she confessed. "I just don't want to be alone. I hate being alone. It's my bane, like a werewolf under the full moon." She unhooked her tail and dropped to the ground.

"I don't understand why Wild Croctail Dragons are the most dangerous creatures ever," Jade said. "Could you educate me? No one explained it."

"Sure!" Sugarbite exclaimed. "It's because of two reasons. First, the only way we can die is because of dragon disease or old age, except for one spot I'm not going to tell you about yet...because anybody might be listening. Second, we have magic venom. It can destroy just about everything except the wall of the Kingdom of Imagination."

"I have two questions."

"Yes?"

"How did Chief Ripsnout get a ripped snout if you can't get hurt?"

"She was a slightly deformed dragonet. Happens all the time."

"Second question: The Kingdom of Imagination has a wall around it?"

"It's a long story. There's a dome of invincible golden thorns way up and that's why you have to use a stormportal to get in and out. Wild Croctail Dragons and Wollions guard it."

"Hmm," Jade said. "That's not what you usually see protecting your average kingdom. How does the government work? Is it just monarchy or something else?"

Sugarbite seemed shocked that Jade thought it was just monarchy. "Of course not!" she ejaculated. "That would give one person too much power."

"Spoken like a true American."

"Instead, there's a Great Council. The King and Queen are a part of the Council. They vote on all major decisions. There's a Council election every time a member of the Great Council died or decided to stop," she blurted out all in one breath.

"Smart," Jade replied.

"Anivia thought it was smart, too."

A rustling sound in the leaves startled them both. A weird bluebird-like creature with a long snout with a horn on the end of it and another bigger horn on its head flapped down. "Hi," he said. "Aren't you Jade, the new Queen?"

"Yes," Jade answered. "What are you and what is your name?"

"I am a Horned Alligator Bluebird," he said. "My name is Shadowspike. Nice to meet you. What's your name?" Shadowspike asked Sugarbite.

"Sugarbite," she said.

"Sounds like a name for something less dangerous than you," he mused. "Was your mother thinking clearly?"

Sugarbite growled. She began to glow.

"What's wrong with you?" Shadowspike questioned.

"Hey Sugarbite, maybe this isn't a good...." Jade began, trying to stop the fight.

It didn't work. Sugarbite glowed brighter and brighter until no one could see. After a large green burst, the light faded. Just like when she had blasted her siblings away, Shadowspike flew backwards. He caught himself in midair and glanced back at the still-glowing dragonet. His eyes wide, he turned and fled into the forest.

"You shouldn't have...." Jade began.

"I know."

"Then why did you do it?"

"I don't know. For some reason, it felt good."

"Felt good?" Jade was going to get to the bottom of why everyone hated creatures with powers—even if it meant challenging Anivia herself.

Chapter Ten:
Flaming Rolls of Toilet Paper

By the appropriate hour on Friday at Starfall, Jade, in her new dress, was almost to the entrance to Ruby Castle. Thousands of creatures were gathered to see her coronation. The Dragon of the Sun and Moon was waiting at the ruby doors.

As she entered, she saw Illuminati wave to her, motioning for her to come forward. He was wearing a tuxedo that had to be one from Sandypool's Clothing Store. Dougal the Demon Mouse was sitting on his head.

When she reached Airgor, he said to her, "Jade Alexandra Skystone, do you accept the responsibility to take care of this Kingdom and rule it fairly?"

"I do," Jade replied.

Airgor reached for a velvet pillow behind him and handed her a flask filled with a golden liquid. "Drink it," he whispered.

She raised the flask to her lips and took a sip. Power and warmth surged through her. The pinpoint of the power was in the center of her forehead. A line came out of the pinpoint and swirled up around her head, letting out a hiss of air. Jade felt the snake crown blink. After a couple seconds, the Ridgeback Rattlesnake crown stilled. It was just like the one on the heads of Kings and Queens in the creepy hall in the tunnels of Tormakk Rock.

"By the powers of Lady Anivia, Jade Skystone is the new ruler of the Kingdom of Imagination! Behold the new Queen!" the Dragon of the Sun and Moon shouted. "Long live the Queen!"

"Long live the Queen!" the crowd roared back.

Cannons on the spires of Ruby Castle fired. Instead of a cannonball, flaming rolls of toilet paper were blasted into the air. Confetti rained down. Large cakes were rolled into sight.

"All right, who put the toilet paper rolls in *this* time?" Airgor raged.

As Jade walked back down the steps, reporters swarmed her.

"Where did you get that beautiful dress?" one asked.

"Sandypool's Clothing Store in Hada," she replied.

The reporter jotted down her answer before being pushed out of the way by a dragon that looked like the one that had flown over Jade's head when she was going back to the hut from buying a dress.

"What do you think your first act as Queen will be?" the dragon asked.

"I don't know," she answered.

The next reporter looked like a rainbow brontosaurus. "Why do you think you will be a good Queen?"

"Because I can understand feelings, and that's really useful when you're around a large population that looks to you for guidance," she responded randomly.

"I like that," the rainbow reporter smiled as she scribbled down the answer.

Jade made her way over to a quieter side of the reporters, where she had seen Meadow trying to get close.

"Hi," Meadow said breathlessly as soon as she got close. "It's so hard to get close with this mob. I was watching the coronation from above. Were you nervous?"

"Heck yes!"

"I would have been, too."

Reporters still asked Jade questions, but she ignored them. She hadn't talked to Meadow since Tuesday, and she had wanted to find out what she'd been doing.

"So, what have you been up to?" Jade asked her.

"Not much," she replied. "Mostly work. You?"

"Did the Dragon of the Sun and Moon tell you about my time in the tunnels?"

"No, he only told us you had completed the Trials. Us *Plathai* edit the Kingdom paper! But don't worry, it's probably a long story, and we don't want anyone to overhear."

"Okay, good. Wait, why shouldn't we tell anyone?"

"Because the King or Queen is only allowed to tell close friends what happened down there. And yes, Airgor is included, as well as Lady Anivia."

"Oh, what about large old snakes with no eyes?"

"Excuse me?"

"Nothing."

Howler managed to bound over to them after several attempts and letting loose several fearsome roar—the crowd had not thinned. "How are you doing?" he asked. "Nice dress."

"Thanks," Jade replied.

"Hey, Howler! We haven't been able to talk at all lately! What have you been doing?" Meadow exclaimed. "Did you actually groom all of your fur for once?"

"It was a special event!"

"And did you sharpen your claws?"

"Maybe!" He smiled mischievously. "Did you clean your feathers?"

"I do that every day!"

"I think you're in love," Jade added in.

"Be quiet!" Meadow and Howler said in unison.

"That is no way to talk to your Queen," she replied, standing up a bit straighter.

They all burst out laughing. It was fun, just hanging out together by the fountains. Besides all the reporters yelling questions at her, it was awesome.

"I have something funny and very painful to tell you," Meadow giggled. "I was watching this little *Platha*, Mudfluff, learn how to fly yesterday. He finally did it! He was so proud of himself, he looked like he was about to make his smile bigger than his face. But then he kind of forgot to look where he was flying, and went, *smack,* right into a cliff wall! When he lifted his head, he looked so confused. It was hilarious and painful!"

"If only you had a FlyCam," Howler sighed. "You could have sent it to *The Kingdom's Funniest Uh-Oh's*."

"*The Kingdom's Most Hilarious Uh-Oh's*? What's that?" Jade asked.

"Sort of like-what do you call it again? *America's Funniest House Bloopers*?" Meadow tried to explain.

"*America's Funniest Home Videos,*" Jade corrected.

"That's what I meant."

"You were way off."

"Was not."

"Okay, let's just say you were halfway there."

"Deal."

"Hey guys, why don't we get some cake?" Howler suggested.

"Good idea," Jade decided.

They headed over to the tables that held large pyramid cakes. There was chocolate, vanilla, red velvet, dark chocolate, mint, chocolate chip, carrot, Oreo, banana, and even a strange multicolored cake that tasted like a different flavor with each color, according to Howler. Meadow got mint, and Howler got red velvet. Jade ended up getting the multicolored cake.

"Did you get red velvet because you like blood?" Meadow teased Howler.

"I most certainly did not," he replied. "I just like the flavor."

"Right," Meadow snorted.

Illuminati walked over to the trio. "Hi," he said. "How's it going?" He held a plate of chocolate chip cake in his claws.

"Hello," Jade answered.

"Hello," Meadow said. "What's your name?"

"I am Illuminati. What's yours?"

"I'm Meadow, and this is Howler."

"Pleased to meet you." He held out a claw to shake. Howler shook it with his paw, and Meadow raised one of her claws to do the same.

A little creature that looked like a bunny with a really long Mohawk and fangs bounded over. "Queen Jade, it is time for your tour of the castle," she said briskly. "It might take a while, so we have to start early."

"Okay," Jade replied. "See you later, guys."

"See you later," they all responded together.

She walked off with Alien Bunny. "What's your name?" she asked her.

"Racoulleaca," she responded.

"What type of creature are you?"

"A Long-Haired Dragonhopper...any more questions?"

Racoulleaca's tone made it clear she didn't like talking about her personal stuff. She was one of those creatures who hated talking about themselves.

They stepped into Imagination Castle. Jade gasped. The main hall was so big it could fit about five male blue whales, if they were from tail-tip to nose-tip. There were several hundred doors leading off on each side. A long, red carpet with golden lining was spread down the middle. A chandelier the size of a Toyota Highlander Hybrid made of mind-reading crystals hung from the high ceiling.

"About half of those doors are for staff," Racoulleaca said in her boring voice. "The other doors are for everything else in the castle that I don't want to explain."

Racoulleaca led her through a wooden door and up a set of stairs spiraling up. At the top was a hallway with two doors on each side. They were marked with little gold plates.

One read, THE KING AND QUEEN. Across from that one read, THE DRAGON OF THE SUN AND MOON.

"How does he even *fit* in there?" Jade asked.

"Magic," Racoulleaca replied. "Haven't you learned already that this place is full of it?"

The gold plate next to her room read UPIR.

"Sweet!" Jade exclaimed. "I live next door to Upir."

"What? You know and like him?" Racoulleaca asked. "He's horrible...sneaking up on everyone and scaring them. Some say they need to tie a bell around his neck. *I* say he needs eyes."

"If you get to know him, he's not bad," Jade snapped. "He's quite nice, actually."

Racoulleaca snorted. "Right, and I'm a Giant Woodpecker Snake. Anyway, this is your room." She stood up on her hind legs and turned the knob. They walked inside. There was a large queen-sized bed, lots of furniture, a makeup table with a mirror, a large closet full of dresses, a dresser, and some paintings of past Kings and Queens.

"Pretty nice, isn't it?" Racoulleaca said dreamily. "It's my favorite room in the castle. Oh, and there's a balcony overlooking two of the five Rivers. The one on the left is Hope, and the one on the right is Strength. The others are Youth, Memories, and Healing. They all flow to Ruby Castle. Only those in dire need of one of them may drink. The little mix you had at your coronation? That was all five Rivers in there."

"Well, isn't that nice. Five magic rivers flowing into this place. Not to be rude or anything, but I think my brain is going to spontaneously combust."

"Also, I hope you still have the map the Wild Croctail Dragons gave you, because I'm only hitting the highlights in this place." Racoulleaca turned and marched out.

"So, what are the highlights we're hitting?" Jade asked.

"You'll see."

Along the wall were several painted pictures. One featured a creature the size of a large chameleon with a beak, talons for front feet, elephant for hind feet, spikes, and a tail that split into two snakes. He was wearing armor. "Who is that?" Jade asked.

"Commander Pocaroo, a Spiked Elephant Snake Bird— he died in the First War."

"The First War?"

"When the Darkness first appeared hundreds of centuries ago, he was banished, and was not seen for several thousand years," Racoulleaca explained impatiently. "Then, out of nowhere, he attacked. That was the Second War. This was the war that killed your parents. After, like before, he vanished like the breeze. Some think he died. Others think he's going to strike again, but with more power. And most of all, he wants to destroy the Royal Family. So, naturally, you are his target."

"Joy and cupcakes."

A door opened, and a creature the size of a horse with a whip-thin tail, the head of a cat, and the hands and feet of a lemur walked out.

"Hello," Jade said. "What's your name?"

"I am Aiko, a Long-Tailed Lemur Cat. I work in the kitchen," she replied. She held out a hand to shake. "You must be Queen Jade."

Jade shook it. "I must be," she agreed.

Aiko and Racoulleaca's eyes met. Something in their eyes flashed between them. It reminded Jade of the feeling she received when the older kids in the orphanage teamed up. It unsettled her a lot, but she couldn't think of why.

And then it hit her.

The thing in their eyes meant they were planning something evil.

Chapter Eleven:
Upir + Googly Eyes = BOOM

Racoulleaca showed the new queen the Dining Hall, the kitchen, the throne room, the ballroom, and much more. By the time they had finished the tour, it was late. Racoulleaca sent Jade to her room to get some sleep.

Her Ridgeback Rattlesnake crown would not come off, no matter how hard she pried. Eventually, she looked at her bed and realized there was a strange indent in the wood that was carved like it was supposed to hold a crown.

She crashed onto the blue, fluffy bed and stuck the crown in its hole. Her feet were sore from walking up and down and all around. *Lights out*, she thought. The crystal lights dimmed, then went out.

However much she tried, though, she just tossed and turned, worried about what Racoulleaca and Aiko were planning. Finally, she managed to slip into an uneasy sleep. But her dreams were plagued with nightmares.

Jade was standing in the same cave-like place as her previous nightmare. Instead of one chamber, there were five.

The first was filled with water. It contained a water creature with an elephant trunk, deer legs instead of pectoral fins that had a webby substance connecting them to the body, a dorsal fin, and the tail of a shark. The poor guy was banging around his tank, yelling death threats with a lot of bad words to the Darkness.

The second chamber had a creature the size of a horse with the head of a bird, horns, four talons connected to each other like a sugar glider, and a lion-like tail with little flaps on the sides of the tip. He was also yelling creatively at the Darkness.

The third held a creature with the head of a dog, a unicorn horn, wings, four talons, and a barbed tail. She was curled up, every breath shaking her body.

The fourth contained a two-legged ostrich with no wings and the head of a Loch Ness Monster. He was running around in circles, yowling as loud as he could.

The fifth also lived in water. She was actually a Loch Ness Monster. She swam silently, but Jade could tell she was terrified.

Over in a corner stood the creature Gredra. The Darkness was next to her. He said something she couldn't make out. Gredra pulled the lever once again, and black filled the cages.

It was horrible to watch five more innocent creatures become slaves to the Darkness. Once the process was complete, Gredra pulled another lever, and the bottoms of the chambers lowered onto a large field where an army of black creatures was being assembled.

Jade took one look at the growing army and decided to try and get out of the nightmare. Luckily, a large, angry yell entered her ears and woke her up.

She leaped out of bed and threw open the door. Upir was out in the hallway with plastic googly eyes taped to his face.

"I will murder whoever did this!" He thrashed around, trying to get it off, which was unsuccessful considering they were taped to his face.

Jade rushed out the door. "Calm down!" she ordered. "Just calm down a little and I'll get them off!"

She managed to get the googly eyes off fairly quickly. That was good because otherwise, he would have awakened the entire castle with his banging and shouting. Once he settled down, she asked him how it had happened.

"I don't know!" he said furiously. "I woke up, looked in the mirror, and saw I had them on!"

All of a sudden, a puffing Demon Mouse came scurrying down the hallway. "Queen Jade!" she squeaked. "Come quick! The Dragon of the Sun and Moon wouldn't tell me what was going on exactly, but he said to hurry!"

"What?" Jade thought about her dream. What if it was about the missing creatures in the dark cave?

"Come now!" the little Demon Mouse said frantically. Then she turned and ran off, with Jade at her heels.

They raced down the spiral stairs—the Demon Mouse sliding down the rail of a miniature set—and ran towards the Dragon of the Sun and Moon, who was pacing the main hall.

He galloped over to her. "There are five missing creatures. All of them were good, and were at their houses last night. And then...."

"Poof," Jade said. "Listen, I had a dream...."

She explained her dream. When she finished, he sat down on his haunches. "That is very disturbing," he said. "You're telling me exactly what happened to them."

"And that's not the worst part," Jade warned grimly. "He's building an army of entirely black creatures."

"The Army of Dark Creatures is rising?" Airgor muttered. "That is very bad. The Darkness is active again."

"What should we tell the Kingdom?" she asked.

"We must keep it a secret for now," he replied sadly. "After all, it was only ten years ago the Second War ended. We cannot place a fear in so soon. It will take at least several years to get a fairly good army."

"But we can't tell them only when the Darkness is ready!" Jade argued. "We won't be prepared; we'll just be dropping a bomb and running away! We can't do that to the Kingdom!"

"It's for their own good. I swore an oath to always put the safety of my Kingdom first, and I will keep it."

"If it's for their safety, then tell them the truth! They have to be prepared!"

"They will panic! I know what to do. Just be patient until we come up with a good plan!"

"And who is making this plan? You?"

"No, the Great Council will come up with a plan."

"I thought you said we couldn't tell anybody what was going on!"

"I meant everyone except for the Great Council. Come on." He turned and tromped down the long hall, down to the door leading to the throne room, where the Great Council discussed important matters. Jade had to run to keep up.

When the Dragon of the Sun and Moon reached the door, he shrunk down to the size of a horse. Together, he and Jade stepped into the throne room.

The entire council was assembled. At the other side sat a golden throne studded with precious stones. Jade went and sat on the throne, as Racoulleaca instructed her to do the previous day. Airgor took his seat beside her.

There were thirteen possible Council members: The King and/or Queen, Airgor, and ten others who varied, depending on who the Kingdom voted on. In front of each Council member was a little gold nameplate stating their name and type of creature.

The member on the far right of the throne was a Brontodragon. His name was Bigtail.

The member next to him was a four-legged vulture with a dog tail. His name was Swoop. The gold nameplate said he was a Vulture Dog.

After him sat a small, lizard-sized creature with wings, the face of a fox, and the body of a horned lizard. Her name was Hestia. She was a Flying Lizard Fox.

Next to Hestia, swimming in a floating water tank, was an eel with a head on its tail. He swam in the shape of a horseshoe. His name was Dolphark. Below was printed his species: a Double Electric Eel.

The last member on the right side was tiny. She was so small she was behind a magnifying glass. She looked like the result of a pig and spider breeding: eight hairy pig legs, little fangs, a pig snout, and pig ears. She looked like a Brazilian Wandering Spider, the deadliest kind in the world. Her name was Miranda. She was classified as a Spiderpig.

On the far left of the throne was the same species as the two-legged Loch Ness Monster-headed no-winged ostrich in Jade's dream. Her name was Windrunner. She was a Loch Ness Ostrich.

The member next to Windrunner had the upper body of a human, the lower body of a snake, fangs, and wings. At the tip of his tail was a stinger dripping venom. He was a Snake Person with the name of Lucifer. He looked like a General Patton who was about to yell about using their enemies' guts for grease on their tank tread.

Beside Lucifer sat a Horned Lionsnake. Her name was Mirtera.

Next to Mirtera was a large water creature with a unicorn horn, two dorsal fins, a shark tail, two pectoral fins, and the head of a Thalassomedon. His name was Barnacle, and looked very old and grumpy. He was a Sea Unicorn Brontosaurus.

On the left, right next to the throne sat a brown, medium-sized dragon with a spiky ball on the end of her tail. Her name was Muddywings. She was an Earth Dragon.

"Something terrible has happened," Airgor started. "Besides Hora the Wollion, we have five missing creatures: Whitecap the Deer-Footed Elephant Shark, Sunbolt the Sugar Glider Bird, Heavenfeather the Spiked Unicorn Dird, Strongkick the Loch Ness Ostrich, and Coral the Loch Ness Monster. Queen Jade knows what happened to them."

This was Jade's cue to pick up the talking. "I had a dream the Army of Dark Creatures was rising. In the dream, all five of the missing creatures were in chambers. Someone named Gredra pulled a lever and turned them evil. Then, she lowered them onto the field where the army was assembling."

"Gredra?" Miranda exclaimed. "That traitor!"

"Yeah!" Bigtail agreed. "What did the Kingdom ever do to her?"

The Dragon of the Sun and Moon interrupted them. "We need to come up with a plan that will protect the rest of the Kingdom, but doesn't tell them what's going on. Any ideas on how to do this without inspiring mass panic?"

"We could make more Wild Croctail Dragons defend the borders," Lucifer suggested. "More border patrol, more defense, safer Kingdom."

"Forcing them to be soldiers?" Muddywings snorted. "I think not! If you knew anything about any type of dragons, you should know they're more stubborn than a little kid who won't eat his vegetables!"

"We could pretend that one of our scopes has spotted traces of the Darkness," Barnacle spoke up. "Our most trusted scope could keep the secret."

"And then we wouldn't have to tell the Kingdom what exactly was going on!" Swoop added on excitedly. "We could exaggerate the truth, and be on Lookout Lockdown. This way, we won't have to say that someone is missing!"

The other Council members nodded in agreement.

"Okay," Jade decided. "All those in favor of Barnacle and Swoop's plan, say, 'Aye'!"

"Aye!" the entire Great Council replied together.

"Ladies and gentlemen," Jade said, "I believe we have ourselves a plan."

Jade assigned jobs to the Council members. Lucifer suggested they tell Arkan the Spiked Elephant Snake Bird their plan. Windrunner, who was the fastest, went to go tell him. Dolphark swam over to the press room in his floating water bubble to tell them what Arkan had "spotted." Bigtail tromped down to the Security room to initiate Lookout Lockdown mode. Muddywings and Jade went to the newsroom to tell the entire Kingdom at one time what exactly was going on.

Muddywings was usually on the news, so she and Jade were voted to go. Once they were there, Muddywings sat down at a computer, typed something up, and printed it. Handing it to Jade, she said, "Hope you are good at reading script. Stick to it. There's no rehearsal, so don't mess up."

"That's just wonderful!"

There was a Snag cameraman in the filming room. His name was Seymore. When he gave them the thumbs up, they began.

Jade looked down at her script. "Creatures of the Kingdom of Imagination," she began, "one of our scopes has spotted traces of the Darkness. We are initiating Lookout Lockdown mode."

"Do not be alarmed. No need to panic," Muddywings added. "It was only a sighting, only as close as 90,000 light years away. The farthest it could have been 95,000 light years away. Again, do not be alarmed. There is no need to panic."

"And now for our daily weather report," Jade read. The camera turned off, and they got up. As they walked out of the newsroom, Muddywings told Jade, "Good job. Have you ever done something like that?"

"Never," she admitted. "Usually, I hate being on camera. Especially in front of a large group of people. But it was short and sweet."

"You were pretty amazing for doing it a first time," Muddywings replied.

"Meh," Jade told her. "Inside, I was petrified like a Medusa victim."

They went back to the Great Council meeting room. By the time they got there and took their seats, everyone else was back.

"Arkan agreed to the plan immediately," Windrunner reported.

"I told you he would," Lucifer said smugly.

"And the press typed it out immediately and sent it to the *Plathai* for editing," Dolphark added. "It'll be out later today."

Bigtail said, "Lookout Lockdown is initiated. I ran the system, and there were no problems. Everything was working perfectly."

"Good," Jade said. "Did you make sure someone was constantly checking on it to make sure there are no problems?"

"I ran into Racoulleaca, and she said she'd take turns with Aiko. I trust them to do the right thing, and I know they will."

That bit of news unsettled her. She wasn't completely positive the two friends were entirely trustworthy. What if they were involved with the kidnapping? Should she tell the Great Council of her suspicions? But what if they really were innocent?

She decided it could wait.

Chapter Twelve:
A Dream a Day
Will Cause an Entire Kingdom to Panic

Two nights later, Jade had another nightmare. This time, in one of the four chambers, she recognized a Banded Lemur Bird. It was Monkey. He was banging around, trying to break the thick glass.

In the next chamber was a dragon that looked like the one who had been soaring around the moon when she had been coming back from dinner with Illuminati. She was very pretty, with a sideways, fuller crescent moon on her head and tail and sparkling stars on her scales. She was breathing a black and silver type of fire. Apparently, the glass was immune to melting as well as shattering.

After her was a water creature that had the horn that pterodactyls have on the back of her head and a long, eel-like body. She kept leaping up out of the water to try and pop the lid on the chamber.

In the fourth chamber was a tiny creature with butterfly wings, butterfly body, a hornet stinger, and a strange head. He was flying all around the chamber, looking for a way out.

Once again, the Darkness gave the command, and Gredra pulled the lever. And once again, the innocent creatures were turned evil and lowered onto the field.

The army seemed twice as big as it looked two nights ago. The fact they could multiply so quickly was extremely bad. There were so many weapons, some being passed out, it could've supplied all of China's army, navy, and air force.

When Jade woke up, she got dressed and knocked on Airgor's door. He must have known something was very wrong, because he called a Council meeting before she even had time to explain what she had seen.

Once everyone had arrived, Jade explained what she had seen. As soon as she finished, everyone started freaking out.

Miranda was the calmest. "If they have enough weapons to supply China's army, navy, and air force, we're in trouble!" she screamed at the top of her lungs.

"We're all going to die!" Dolphark wailed.

"He's got to be attacking the other Kingdoms!" Swoop screeched.

"We have to prepare an army immediately, lest we are all consumed by the shadows!" Hestia yowled. "Anivia! Save us!"

"Sileeeeeeeeence!" Airgor's voice echoed through the meeting room, causing everyone to be quiet and sit back down. "You are brave Council members who the Kingdom voted to save them from evil times such as these," he snarled. "What would the Kingdom do if they found out you're as scared as worms are of birds?"

A few of the members looked ashamed.

"Now," Airgor continued, but in a much less chew-you-out-for-being-a-coward tone, "Let's discuss who was taken. Monkey the Banded Lemur Bird, Crescent the Vampire Moon Dragon, Abalone the Pterodactyl Eel, and Buzz the Fanged Butterfly Hornet."

"What do we do now?" Lucifer asked.

"Well, obviously, try and find what cave they were in," Windrunner declared. "Without that important little bit of information, we have no way to spy on them."

"True," Barnacle agreed. "But how do we do that?"

"We could follow them," Muddywings suggested.

That's a good idea, except for one little flaw, Jade thought. *How can we follow someone who we don't know and could literally kidnap someone anywhere? IN AN ENTIRE KINGDOM?*

"How? It's not like we can track every single creature so we know which one cave in the entire universe they're being taken to," Swoop pointed out.

An idea suddenly popped into Jade's head. "Actually, we can," she said.

Everyone turned to look at her.

"We can sneak tracking devices into everyone's food. We can do it to every food place. This way, it can't be taken out except with surgery, which is highly unlikely, because the Darkness won't notice it until someone gets there."

"Wow," Miranda said faintly. "Except one thing: how can we mass produce trackers without anyone noticing?"

Jade's heart sunk...she had not thought about that.

"But," she continued, "maybe we can figure out who his next target is."

"Miranda, you are a genius!" Bigtail shouted. "Maybe he left DNA of his next targets somehow!"

"How would he do that, though?" Swoop asked. "He'd have to, like, touch them. Also, how would we know where to look?"

"Well, then, I guess that's out of question," Airgor said. "But we can figure out what his previous targets had in common and see what he's looking for. Barnacle, will you make one of your famous charts, please?"

While they waited for Barnacle to finish his chart of missing creatures, they discussed what the creatures' traits were.

"Whitecap was a soldier from the Second War," Mirtera remembered. "A common soldier, only cared about his home, family, and friends. He would defend it with his life."

"I'm pretty sure Sunbolt was a baker," Swoop said, squinting at a musty old scroll. "And it says here that Heavenfeather ran an entertainment company."

"I used to know Strongkick when I was little. We were in the same class." Windrunner sighed. "He was a good fellow. He grew up to be a nice social worker."

"Coral was a principal," Dolphark said. "My cousin's kid went to her school."

"Monkey was my friend's friend," Jade said sadly. "I really hope Illuminati doesn't miss him too badly."

"Who's Illuminati?" Windrunner asked.

"He's a Bi-Mouth Tri-Ocular Dragicorn."

"Oh."

"I don't think we really know anything big about Crescent," Miranda said thoughtfully. "But if she's anything like the other Vampire Moon Dragons, she'd have probably been taken during the middle of the day, when she's sleeping."

"And that's the biggest mystery," Swoop said. "Because some nocturnal creatures change sleeping habits to go to certain amusement parks that close before they wake up."

"Let's come back to her," Dolphark suggested.

"So, what about Abalone?" Jade asked. "Does anyone know her?"

Everyone shook their head.

"Maybe I could check the scroll again," Swoop suggested. "It has a lot of creatures' jobs." He unrolled the old scroll again, scanning the list of A's under the JOB section.

"Here she is," he said, pointing at a name on the scroll. "She worked in an Investment Council. And here's Buzz! He was a doctor in Bugville. Also, here's Hora: she's a fighter for her Prack."

"All once good, fair citizens turned evil," Airgor said.

"I finished." Barnacle's creaky voice silenced them. They all rushed and crowded around to see the amazing chart that he had drawn.

Hora
Fighter
Mother and father dead, fought in Second War
Likes to entertain cubs with war stories that her parents told her
Species: Wollion

Whitecap
Soldier in Second War
Very brave
Cared about the Kingdom
Likes to tell war stories
Species: Deer-Footed Elephant Shark

Sunbolt
Baker
Dad a former soldier
Always helping out
Made donations for orphans
Species: Sugar Glider Bird

Heavenfeather
Runs Entertainment Co.
Actor for company
Babysits
Aunt and Uncle fought in Second War
Species: Spiked Unicorn Bird

Strongkick

Social Worker
Brother a current soldier
On the Rebfin Red Hots soccer team
Species: Loch Ness Ostrich

Coral
Principal at Swisher School
Mother killed, on the side of the Darkness
Likes to read in free time
Species: Loch Ness Monster

Monkey
Farmer
Oldest sister a soldier, died in Second War
Likes to be outside
Species: Long-Tailed Lemur Bird

Crescent
Teaches flying to dragonets
Both parents died in Second War
Likes to do night flying
Species: Vampire Moon Dragon

Abalone
Investment advisor
Sister killed, on side of the Darkness
Likes to tell funny stories to kids
Species: Pterodactyl Eel

Buzz
Doctor
Mother dead, fought in Second War
Likes to make checkups fun
Species: Fanged Butterfly Hornet

Jade finished reading. "That's really useful," she said. "Thanks, Barnacle!"

"Hmm," Swoop thought. "It looks like he's targeting everyone with connections to the Second War, which would be hard to sort out from everyone else. Nearly everyone in the entire Kingdom either is or related to a soldier."

"So not completely useful," Hestia supplied. "Not for current purposes, anyway."

"How about this?" Airgor suggested. "Queen Jade and I contact Lady Anivia while the rest of you contact the other Kingdoms?"

"Good idea," Bigtail exclaimed.

"Yes," echoed Dolphark.

"Let's do it," agreed Windrunner.

"Hold on a second." Jade frowned. "There are more Kingdoms?"

"Three others, to be exact," Miranda said kindly. "The Kingdom of the Superverse, the Kingdom of Tribes, and the Kingdom of Three Queens—all have their own god or goddess. All just as well protected as ours."

"Okay, those in favor of the plan I just suggested, say, 'Aye!'" Airgor interrupted.

"Aye!" repeated the rest of the Great Council.

"Well, then," Airgor said. "Windrunner, Bigtail! Contact the Kingdom of Three Queens. Dolphark, Hestia, Mirtera! Contact the Kingdom of the Superverse. Miranda, Lucifer, Muddywings! Contact the Kingdom of the Tribes. Barnacle, Swoop, stay here and see if you can find out any more on the kidnappings. Queen Jade, you come with me."

Jade followed the Dragon of the Sun and Moon out and down a long, empty corridor. "Uh, how exactly do we contact a goddess?" she asked him.

"Get her attention." He unlocked the door at the end of the hall, which they had reached. "You'll get a key to this room, too, just in case you have an emergency."

"So, are we going to have to fish for Megalodons or something to get her attention?" Jade wondered.

"Eh," Airgor replied, "not big enough. We're going to use cymbals."

She hoped he was joking.

They stepped inside the room.

Jade suddenly remembered her goal to find out why creatures with powers were resented. *This is how I find out!* She thought. *This is how I can speak to Anivia!*

Chapter Thirteen:
And Peacebringer Was All Like '
Yo Dere, Ya Wanna See Anivia?'

Airgor was not joking. Inside the room was a pair of overlarge cymbals dangling from the ceiling. A long rope was strung to some kind of machine. It seemed to make the cymbals clap together when you pulled it.

He walked over to it. "When clapped together, they will produce a soundwave so high only Anivia can hear it. Then her assistant, Peacebringer, will transport us to The Palace Cloud."

"Okay... So, Lady Anivia has an assistant named Peacebringer and lives in a palace called The Palace Cloud...that's definitely not strange."

"Show some respect." He pulled the rope. The giant cymbals clashed together, but it was impossible to hear. The world began to spin, her necklace began to heat up, and Jade evaporated.

She precipitated in a Grand Hall even bigger than the one in Ruby Castle. A woman in a golden mask with three golden feathers on each side was standing in front of them. Then she unfolded golden, shimmering wings. It was brighter than the sun.

"Hello, Peacebringer," Airgor said.

"Yo, Gor the Charging Boar! Ya here to see Anivia?" Peacebringer sounded like one of those eighties people who was totally groovy.

"Yes, we are," Airgor said patiently. "And it's extremely urgent. So, if you could please...."

"Yeah, sure! Groovy!" Peacebringer replied (Jade's worst suspicions about her were true). She led them across the length of the hall, turned left into another hall, which was a great deal smaller, and in front of an amazing throne that made every other throne look like an old, wooden chair.

The lady on the throne was a whole other story. She didn't have much jewelry or makeup, but she didn't need it. Her hair was the color of almonds. She wore a green robe and a golden Ridgeback Rattlesnake crown like Jade's, as well as a golden star necklace. She literally radiated life. That was the best part about her. Green energy was attracted to her, flowing around her as smoothly as a creek. Just being around her made Jade feel calm.

Of course, this was Anivia, the goddess of the Kingdom of Imagination.

"Greetings, Airgor! Welcome, Queen Jade." Anivia's voice was smoother than molasses. "What can I do for you?"

"We were wondering if you could give us any information at all about the kidnappings," Airgor replied.

Anivia sighed. "I would love to tell you everything: the location of the cave, where they got their army, but alas, *certain rules* restrict me from doing so."

"Which rules?" Jade asked. "You're a goddess, aren't you? Can't you do what you want to?"

Anivia laughed. "Let's say I were to tell you the location of the cave. It is...." She didn't seem to be able to finish the sentence. "See? I have to watch my Kingdom be attacked, and I can't do anything about it. But I am the one who sent those dreams about the growing army of Dark Creatures."

"Is there anything you *can* tell us?" Jade asked.

"Yes," Anivia replied. "They can multiply so quickly because they are creating *Wamekufa*—corpses. They are not completely alive, but not completely dead. More like half and half."

"They're using soldiers from previous wars?" Airgor sounded thoroughly surprised.

"Indeed! This takes a good amount of energy and time, so it happens slowly," Anivia explained. "Technically speaking, we could do it, too, if you could figure out the process. This means that the *Wamekufa* would have to be killed once, and the normal creatures would be killed twice, unless the spell is somehow broken."

"Can you tell us how it can be broken?" Jade pressed.

"Sorry, I wish I could."

"How does the spell work?" the Dragon of the Sun and Moon inquired.

"You need a dead body. It works with any type of inanimate body, not just the kind with the skin still attached. Then you must animate it. Ask Swoop for the rest of the information. He'll know what to do."

"Why him? Has he done it before?" Jade wondered.

"No, but a bookworm like him would definitely like to read the Book of Ancient Spells," Anivia answered.

"Thank you, Lady Anivia." Airgor bowed. His tail nudged Jade, and she followed his example.

"What kind of creature is Gredra?" Jade queried.

Anivia replied, "She, um, is Caraline's twin. They are basically the same except, well, Gredra's evil."

"Well, isn't that nice." Jade was sure her brain was going to crack her skull from growing too much. "The Supreme General of All Armies' twin sister is the Supreme General of All Armies, and of the opposite army, too."

"Is that all I can do for you?" Anivia asked. "Would you like some tea?"

"No, thank you," Airgor said politely. "We should be heading back."

"Okay," Anivia said. "Peacebringer, could you teleport them back?"

"Yeah, of course! See you later, Gor the Charging Boar! Come back soon, Jade That'll Make the Darkness Fade!"

Peacebringer formed a ball of light, just like a miniature sun with all its horribly scorching, burning heat, which Jade and the Dragon of the Sun and Moon were sucked into.

. . . . .

When they returned, everyone except for Windrunner and Bigtail were back. Each went around sharing what had happened.

Miranda, Lucifer, and Muddywings went first. "The Kingdom of the Tribes had no record of missing creatures. Everyone was right where they should be," Lucifer said.

Mirterta, Dolphark, and Hestia went next. "The Kingdom of the Superverse was also free of missing creatures. It seems like only the Kingdom of Imagination is being targeted." Hestia sighed. "That is bad."

"Yes, it is," Windrunner replied. "The Kingdom of Three Queens is not being targeted."

"We know how the Dark Creatures grew so quickly," Jade explained. "They're creating *Wamekufa*—dead soldiers. If we can figure out the spell, we could create our own very large, half dead army. Anivia said that Swoop knew how to do the spell."

Swoop thought for a moment. "Well, there was a library book on spells. It probably had that one in it. Should I go get it?"

"Yes," Dolphark answered. "The sooner we figure out how to do it, the better."

Swoop got up and left. By the time he got back, the Council was discussing who could do the spell. So far, they'd gotten nowhere.

He set the Book of Ancient Spells down and opened it. The book was extremely old and its bindings were fragile. After a few minutes of flipping through the book, Swoop found the spell.

"It's called the Awakening Dead spell. It requires a dead body and someone very strong in the mind-term, meaning they have a strong mind. Next, you repeat the following: 'Dead body in the ground, not meant to be sun-bound, all say amen, you shall live and see the light again!', which should bring back the dead until they die again. The warnings are: Can only be done once per body and can make the caster pass out or go into a weeklong coma if done over and over or in a large group."

Bigtail continued what they had started before Swoop got back. "Does anyone know who is strong in the mind-term? I don't."

"I know one," Swoop volunteered. "Except she's dead."

All of a sudden, Mirtera leaped up, eyes shining. "We could ask my brother's friend Ace!" she exclaimed. "He's a Cheetahphant, and he does meditation, so he should have a strong mind!"

"Brilliant!" Swoop said excitedly. "But can we let him in on our secret?"

"Of course!" Mirtera replied impatiently. "He's one of the most trustworthy Cheetahphants ever!"

"So, who wants to go get him?" Jade asked. "Um, Mirtera, where does he live?"

"He lives right outside the castle's walls in Hadgar. 4955 Savannah Lane, 10347, I think," she answered. "So, not too far away!"

"I'll go get him," Muddywings decided.

"All in favor of Mirtera's plan, say, 'Aye!'" Jade ruled. "And, Muddywings, try not to accidentally club anything with that tail of yours on the way out. We don't want any more broken vase reports!"

"Aye!" the Great Council repeated. "And, Muddywings, try not to accidentally club anything with that tail of yours on the way out. We don't want any more broken vase reports!"

"Oops," Jade apologized. "I did not realize you guys had to say that."

Muddywings flew out of the room. After about half an hour, she returned, with a creature with a trunk, spots, a lightning-shaped tail, two little lightning-shaped ears, and lots of leg muscles in tow.

"Hi, Ace!" Mirtera said, dipping her head to him. "How's your family doing?"

"Fine, thanks." Ace dipped his head to her in return. "And you?"

"I'm doing fine as well," she answered. "Sorry for the short notice of bringing you here. It is a very big emergency."

"No problem," he replied. "What is it?"

"Can you keep an extremely large, important secret?" Jade asked.

"Yes."

"Okay." Jade took a breath. "There was never a sighting of the Darkness. That was completely fake. But there have been several kidnappings: Hora the Wollion, Whitecap the Deer-Footed Elephant Shark, Sunbolt the Sugar Glider Bird, Heavenfeather the Spiked Unicorn Dird, Strongkick the Loch Ness Ostritch, Coral the Loch Ness Monster, Monkey the Long-Tailed Lemur Bird, Crescent the Vampire Moon Dragon, Abalone the Pterodactyl Eel, and Buzz the Fanged Butterfly Hornet."

"Holy Anivia!" Ace exclaimed, eyes wide. " There are *ten* missing creatures?"

"Yes," Jade said gravely. "And that's not the worst part. Their army is giant. They are creating *Wamekufa*, dead soldiers. The only way we can do the spell is if we have someone with a strong mind...that's you."

"Me?" he wondered. "Why me?"

"Because you have a strong mind," Barnacle rasped. He broke off into a coughing fit, sending out a flurry of bubbles. Jade had not realized exactly how old the Sea Unicorn Brontosaurus was.

"What do you need to do the spell?" Ace asked. "Like, what type of preparation do you need?"

"A body and someone strong in the mind-term. Next, you repeat the following: 'Dead body in the ground, not meant to be sun-bound, all say amen, you shall live and see the light again!' But be careful, because if you do too many at once, or continue to do it over and over again in a short period of time, you could either pass out for a little or go into a coma," Swoop ejaculated.

"So, you don't need a lot of practice or anything?" Ace inquired.

"Apparently not," Lucifer said.

"No," Swoop added, looking at the book of spells. "All it requires is a creature strong in the mind-term."

"You might be the only way we can raise the dead to help fight," Jade summarized. "Without your help, it'll be impossible for anyone to ultimately destroy the Darkness once and for all."

"So, are you going to agree? " Mirtera asked. "To save the Kingdom of Imagination from mass destruction?"

Ace sighed. "All right. I will help you."

Chapter Fourteen:
Halloween Should Now Be Every Day

The Great Council meeting ended with the naming of the operation: Emergency Halloween Army. They had agreed to have a meeting every day (with Ace) so they could check up on the progress. Swoop and Barnacle went to help Ace practice the spell. Muddywings, Lucifer, Bigtail, and Windrunner went to go dig up a body or five. Dolphark, Mirtera, Hestia, and Miranda went to find a place to hide their dead soldiers when they turned alive. Airgor went to do his own thing, and Jade went to find Sugarbite to introduce her to Upir.

She walked over to a large creature that was clearly a fire dragon. He looked like a red-hot pepper with an orange belly. With the little red flaps on the tip of his tail to help him steer when he was flying, it looked like his tail was on fire.

"Hi," she said. "I need to get to the Wild Croctail Village. Could you fly me there?"

"Hello, Queen Jade." He bowed. "Of course I can fly you there. Hop on. By the way, my name is Soot."

Jade jumped onto Soot's back, and they flew out a large open window. They soared above Ruby Castle. It gleamed bright red in the noon sunlight. The spires glittered dark pink.

They flew over many towns. Finally, Soot landed in the village. Jade slid down off his back. "Thanks for the lift. I can walk back," she told him.

"No problem! See you later!" He winged off into the distance.

Jade found Spitvenom lapping up water from a small lake. "Hello, Spitvenom!" she said.

Spitvenom looked up at her. "Oh, hello...how are you doing?"

"Fine, thanks," she answered. "And you?"

"I'm okay. My stiff bones are still a pain in the tail," he replied.

"Do you know where Sugarbite might be?" Jade asked the old dragon. "I would like her to meet someone."

"She's climbing trees over there." Spitvenom pointed his snout to a grove of beeches. "I'll tell her mother that she's with you."

"Thanks!" Jade raced towards the trees. "Sugarbite!" she called.

A pine green bundle fell down from one of the branches. "Oof!" Sugarbite exclaimed as she landed in an awkward angle. "Hi! What're you doing here?"

"I want to take you to meet Upir," she responded. "Come on."

"Guess what? I learned how to fly! That's why I couldn't come to your coronation! I was flying!" Sugarbite did a backflip in the air. "Want me to fly you to the castle? Verde said it was good for me to carry weight!"

"Okay," Jade decided. She clambered up onto the little dragon's back. Sugarbite spread her wings and took off.

They crashed through quite a few branches. "Sorry!" Sugarbite yelped. "I haven't completely mastered the forest takeoff yet."

Jade spat out a leaf. "It's okay."

When they reached Ruby Castle, Sugarbite made quite the entrance by crash-landing in the royal garden.

Jade dusted off her clothes. "Come on," she said. "We've got a long walk."

They walked down the main hall and up the set of stairs that led to Jade's room. Jade knocked on Upir's door. It swung open.

"Hello, Queen Jade," Upir said. "Greetings, young Wild Croctail Dragon."

"Hi," Jade replied. "Sugarbite, this is Upir. Upir, this is Sugarbite."

"I'm like you," Sugarbite added. "I'm weird, too."

"Really?" Upir sounded curious, though it was hard to tell, since he could see the future. "What's your power?"

"I glow."

That seemed to take Upir by surprise, but he looked like he was pretending. "You...glow. Okay. That is actually not that strange. There was a Batcat named Sonar in the First War like that, too."

"What's your gift?" Sugarbite asked.

"I can see the past, present, and future of every world. That's why the holes where my eyes should be looks like stars. It resembles the places I see. Want to come inside?"

"Sure," Sugarbite replied immediately.

"I'm going to the library," Jade said. "See you later."

She had said she was going to the library, but instead, she went to the dungeons, where Ace was practicing the Awakening Dead spell.

Jade walked into the dungeon they had chosen. A couple skeletons lay in front of Ace. Barnacle and Swoop had clipboards and were taking notes.

Ace looked up. "Oh, hi," he said. " I've already passed out twice. Check this out! It's wicked!"

He began to chant. "Dead body in the ground, not meant to be sun-bound, all say amen, you will live and see the light again!"

The bones began to clatter. They hovered and were forming a sort of gooey shield around them. It hardened into scales and skin. One looked like the painting of General Pocaroo. Was that his body?

The second looked like a no-legged winged creature with sand-speckled feathers. She had a scorpion stinger on the tip of her tail to go with a mouth full of vicious-looking teeth.

The creature raised her head. Flapping her wings, she managed to hover.

General Pocaroo stood up (Jade was positive that Pocaroo was the name of that creature). He shook himself all over, his eyes blurry. Then he asked confusedly, "What's going on? All I remember is fire and ash and the face of an evil Fire-Breathing Air-Ray before she killed me."

"General Pocaroo, it's okay," Swoop began. "That was a long time ago. It's a long story, so just be patient."

The sand-speckled creature yelped. "Who are you? What's happening? How am I still alive? Where's my sister?"

Barnacle checked his clipboard. "Your name is Aquilina, correct?"

"Yes," Aquilina replied, then repeated, "Where's my sister?"

"What is your sister's name?" Barnacle inquired.

"Grainwing," she answered in a shaky voice. "Have you seen her?"

Barnacle scanned his clipboard. "Sorry," he replied. "She's not on the list."

"W-what do you mean, she's not on the list?" Aquilana's voice quivered.

Swoop carefully twined his tail around her venomous one. "Look," he said sympathetically, "it's difficult to explain. You were...dead for a while. She's dead, too. We brought you back. If you want, we can bring her back, too."

"I was...I was *dead?*"

"Wait," General Pocaroo interrupted. "Was I dead, too?"

"Yes," Swoop responded. "Ace the Cheetahphant over here did the spell."

Ace looked like he was about to fall off his paws. Raising the dead had really taken its toll on the speedster.

"Hi," Ace greeted the newly raised. "I... uh, I'm going to sit down for a while. Anyway, if you two could please follow Barnacle the Sea Unicorn Brontosaurus to the presentation room, that'd be great."

"Thanks for bringing me back," General Pocaroo said as he exited the room.

"Please bring back my sister," Aquilina added.

"Right this way," Barnacle said as he led them out of the room.

"Well, Ace, exactly how many creatures have you brought back from the Underworld?" Jade asked him.

"Oh, those two were my fortieth, I think. Is that correct, Swoop?" Ace said.

"Yes," Swoop confirmed.

"Do you know how hard it is to raise the dead? It's harder than getting a Batcat to sleep during the night!" Ace complained. "Imagine you're drowning, and someone hands you the Declaration of Independence and tells you not to get a drop of water on it! That *is* what it's called, right?"

"Yes," Jade replied. "It sounds hard. What kind of creature is Aquilina?"

"She's a Sand Devil. When she graduated from Galabar School of War, she was instantly promoted to sixth grade Specialist. She was *that* good," Swoop blurted out.

"Sixth Grade Specialist? Am I the only one in this dungeon who doesn't know what that means?"

"Don't worry," Ace assured her. "I don't know what the heck that is, either."

Swoop sighed. "Honestly, has anyone else in this Kingdom read the Guide to the Army and the history of every creature who ever lived?"

"Two things," Ace answered. "One, most creatures don't spend all of their time with their snouts shoved into a book or scroll or some other form of tree. Two, dude! The fact that you know everyone in this Kingdom, alive or dead, like your best friend is just plain *creepy*!"

"Excuse me?" Swoop sounded offended. "I do not spend all of my time with a form of tree in front of my face! For example, I am here helping you!"

Ace raised an eyebrow. "Correct me if I'm wrong, but is that not a piece of paper attached to your clipboard that you are staring onto right now? And I bet if the Darkness ever got in here you would try and research everything about him!"

"Point taken," Swoop admitted.

That reminded Jade about how Bigtail had left Racoulleaca and Aiko on guard duty. Should she tell them? Or should she wait until they did something? *By the time they do something, the Darkness could be invading. Better tell them now.*

"I don't completely trust Racoulleaca and Aiko," Jade started. "When Racoulleaca was giving me the tour, something passed between them. Something that I had seen in Healy Orphanage. It means that they were planning something bad."

"Are you bonkers?" Swoop gasped. "That's crazy! They would never do that!"

"I believe her," Ace objected. "And 'bonkers' and 'crazy' mean the same thing."

"Whatever," Swoop snorted. "But why do you think they would betray their Kingdom and help some supreme evil superpower kill everybody?"

"It's...it is hard to explain," Jade explained. "I just know. I can guarantee they are evil. Bigtail made a bad mistake by leaving them on guard duty."

"I'm still not positive I agree with you. The way *I* heard it, this suspicion is a gut feeling," Swoop argued. "It sounds like you have an inner rattlesnake tail that rattles whenever you meet someone untrustworthy."

"Sort of like that," Jade agreed. "But I know I'm right."

"Fine," Swoop sighed. "But let's go over it with the Great Council. Come on."

"Should I come?" Ace wondered, jumping up.

"No, you should probably stay here for a while," Jade reasoned. "I don't think you can walk up ten flights of stairs."

"Too true." Ace sat back down.

Swoop and Jade left the dungeon and headed up to the meeting room. Before they reached the last set of stairs, however, an oversized panther like creature with wings, a scorpion tail, and a whole lot of muscles nearly crashed into them.

"Sorry," he gasped. "Were you going to the meeting room?"

"Yes," Jade replied. "What's going on?"

"Something horrible has just happened!" he howled. "Racoulleaca and Aiko have just opened the gates of the Kingdom of Imagination and then they disappeared!"

Chapter Fifteen:
Why Is It So Hard
to Stop an Entire Kingdom from Dying?

"Treachery!" the panther creature roared. "And the Darkness is getting closer!"

"Wait," Jade said. "Couldn't someone just go into the Control Room and just turn Lookout Lockdown mode back on?"

"No!" he answered. "No one can get in! They have somehow barred the doors so no one can get through!"

"Okay." Jade thought quickly. "Calm down. What's your name and what kind of creature are you?"

"My name is Stormplume," he answered. "I am a Flying Panther. We must get into the Control Room and turn on Full Lockdown Mode!"

"Have you asked Airgor to ram against it as hard as he can?" Jade asked desperately. "Maybe he can break in somehow."

"I was about to ask him," Stormplume replied. "I'll go get him!"

He flew off. Moments later, he returned with the Dragon of the Sun and Moon right behind him.

Stormplume was out of breath again, but Airgor was the complete opposite. He was so angry he looked like a gold, silver, and purple devil emoji. "Let's go," he grunted when he and Stormplume reached them.

They raced towards the Control Room at the very top floor, where hundreds of creatures, all staff of the castle, were crowded around the door.

"Everybody get back!" Airgor roared. Once they did, he asked the staff to open the roof. The Fire Dragon who had flown Jade to the Wild Croctail Village soared up and pulled back a sliding window, letting sunlight stream through.

Airgor began to concentrate. His spirals began to glow as bright as a solar eclipse. Well, it wasn't *that* bright, since if it had been as bright as a solar eclipse, they would've all gone blind.

He was clearly using Lunar Twilight Magic. Once he was all "charged up," he galloped full speed at the Control Room doors.

The doors were blasted open like they were hit with a bazooka. As soon as the doorway was cleared, a creature with two snake heads, the body of a horse, and a dog tail rushed forward and slammed her hoof onto a large red button that read, FULL LOCKDOWN MODE! EMERGENCIES ONLY!

Red lights popped out of the walls and began to light up and spin like sirens. A golden glow appeared directly north of the open ceiling and spread like a ripple, then faded.

"Go check the position of the Darkness," Airgor growled to a Rhinolion who was clearly a part of the "Darkness Lookout Crew." The Rhinolion nodded and raced off.

About fifteen minutes later, he burst back into the hall. "Getting closer and closer," he wheezed, "and growing rapidly."

And then everyone died.

Well, it only *looked* like everyone died. About half the creatures fainted. The rest ran around screaming, panicking, and basically causing mass destruction by running over everything in their path...including each other.

"Well, that's just great," Airgor grumbled. "I think it's your turn to get them to calm down."

"Why me?" Jade asked. "You're much louder, and you're much more, um, *experienced* with that stuff." What she was really thinking was *You're older, you should do it.*

He must've read her mind or something, because he answered, "Just because I'm older doesn't mean I should always be the one to calm them down every time. You're their Queen. They'll do what you tell them to do."

"Fine," she replied. "But it will most likely fail."

"Humph," came the response.

Jade cupped her hands around her mouth and yelled, "EVERYONE CALM DOWN!"

All the creatures turned to stare at her.

Well, Jade thought, *that worked.*

"Okay, listen up," she commanded when everyone had settled down. "Here's what's going to happen. You there!" She pointed to an ash-black dragon with strange wings that only had the bone part of the wings and a crooked tail. "Alert the Wild Croctail Dragons. And you!" she pointed to a Banded Lemur Bird. "There's a Cheetahphant named Ace in the dungeons. Tell him what's going on, and then tell him to continue what he was doing earlier, and to hurry."

The dragon and the Banded Lemur Bird bounded off.

Jade turned to the Rhinolion. "Show me the Darkness," she commanded.

"This way," he replied, legs still shaking from fear. His fur was so puffed up he looked like a large, brown-and-gray, extremely fluffy pillow. He led her down a corridor and into an observatory room.

"This is how we see outside the Kingdom," the Rhinolion explained, pointing to a very large telescope. "Go ahead and take a look."

Jade peered through the eyehole of the telescope. In the distance, she saw the blackness she had come to associate with death growing closer and bigger by the minute. The Darkness must have been gathering his army of dead creatures for the attack. Quickly doing some math, she realized they could be ready to attack in about thirty minutes, and after that, they would arrive in about in an hour.

"This is *extremely* bad," she murmured. "What's your name?"

"I'm Boulder," he answered. "What in the name of Anivia are we going to do? The Darkness has a massive army!"

"So do we," Jade responded. "Or, we will. Long story. I've got to go."

"Wait," Boulder called. "Where are you going?"

But Jade had already left. When she reached the dungeon, the Banded Lemur Bird was already leaving.

"Oh, hello Queen Jade," he said, then... "Bye." He ran up the cold stone stairs, probably to get his family to safety.

Ace was apparently about to do a spell when she dashed into the room. "What's up?" he asked. "I am trying very hard not to panic, because if I do, I can't do the spell. Could you get someone to dig up some bodies for me?"

Jade almost laughed, had it not been for the fact they were all about to be consumed by an unstoppable evil creature that wanted to take over the Kingdom of Imagination. "That would be a pleasant chat. 'Hello, would you mind digging up some ancient skeletons and hauling them down to the dungeons?'"

Ace actually smiled, despite the trouble they were in. "Maybe you could ask someone we know?"

"On it," she replied. "See you later. Try not to pass out!" She ran out of the dungeon and up the stairs.

As she dashed around the castle, she bumped into Muddywings, who looked like she'd just run a marathon with zombies behind her.

"Sorry," she wheezed when she ran into Jade.

"I'm so glad I ran into you, actually," Jade responded. "Could you do me a favor?"

"Sure, if it leads up to destroying the Darkness," Muddywings answered. "What is it?"

"I need you to dig up some bodies and bring them down to Ace," Jade explained. "It'll get you pretty dirty, but it's important."

"Okay." Muddywings shuddered. "If you or anyone needs me, I'll be in the army cemetery."

She hurried out onto a balcony. Spreading her brown, scaly wings, she launched herself into the Middlesun sky.

Jade rushed up to the Control Room again. The crowd of terrified creatures had thinned greatly. She suspected Airgor had ordered them back to their normal duties and routines.

She found the Dragon of the Sun and Moon sitting in front of the large window that viewed half of the Kingdom.

"I had asked you to calm them down," he rumbled. "Did you find anything big or important out?"

"No," Jade admitted. "But I asked Muddywings to bring some corpses down to Ace for re-animation."

"Good idea," Airgor replied. "We should be as prepared as possible when the Darkness begins to attack. And the Wild Croctail Dragons are getting into position."

In the distance, a green cloud of Wild Croctail Dragons soared upward towards the sky. Then, all of a sudden, they vanished in a flash of golden light. Apparently, the dome sucked up creatures who needed to guard the gates and brought them just outside of the wall.

This reminded her of Sugarbite and Upir. She doubted that Sugarbite knew about the attack. Upir would probably warn her, though.

She decided to check on them anyway. "I'll be right back," Jade responded. "I just have to check on someone."

"You're running all over the castle," Airgor grunted. "I heard you brought in a guest this morning. Are you going to check on her?"

"Yes."

"Be quick. When you come back, go do the news."

"Should I get Muddywings?"

"Nah, you know the ropes. Do it by yourself."

Jade raced out of the Control Room. Dashing through crisscrossing hallways, she accidentally knocked over a table, stood it back up, and kept on running. When she reached Upir's room, she slammed her fist three times onto the dark oak wood.

The door swung open. Sugarbite said, "If it's about the attack, I know already. Upir told me as soon as it happened."

Upir slithered behind her. "It turns out we have a lot in common."

"You should probably stay here, Sugarbite," Jade decided. "I don't want you flying around when there could be an attack."

"They couldn't hurt me," Sugarbite snorted.

"But they could capture you," Upir warned, "and stick a pointy thing into your weak spot. And put you in a cage with a secret formula to make you evil."

"What!" Sugarbite almost jumped out of her scales. "They can *do* that?"

"Long story," Jade replied. "Just stay here with Upir. Don't leave the castle unless you really have to."

"Okay." Sugarbite's voice quivered a little.

Jade rushed downstairs to the newsroom. The Snag at the camera had clearly been suspecting she would come, and had already typed out a pretty nice script for her to use.

"Thanks," she said.

Eyes were wide with fear of being slaughtered by the Darkness; his only response was a friendly nod.

Skimming over the script, she asked, "Did you come up with this by yourself?"

"Yes," he answered.

"That's cool! I don't believe I caught your name. What is it?"

"My name is Rocky."

"Nice name."

"Thank you. Should I prepare the camera?"

"Yes, that would be great."

She sat on her stool and waited.

Rocky pointed a claw in her direction when he had the camera rolling.

Jade looked down at her script. She read, "Creatures of the Kingdom of Imagination. If you are to panic with this message, do it calmly. Two staff of Ruby Castle have opened the gates to the Kingdom and barred the doors. The Darkness is getting closer. Luckily, we were able to force open the doors. Unluckily, however, the Darkness is still right out there. We have more guards guarding the gates. Do whatever you can to protect yourselves. All we know is that the Darkness wants to get in here, and he won't stop. We will be distributing Healing water. However, there is only enough for one cup per creature. Use it wisely. Please do not let fear turn you into creatures who fight over simple things. Stay safe. Be nice. And don't panic too much."

Rocky shut the camera off. "Great job," he complimented her. "I considered doing it myself, but I'm not very convincing. I hope they listen to you, because they might not listen to anyone else."

"I hope so, too," Jade agreed. "That would be really bad."

They stood in an awkward silence for a couple moments. Jade broke the silence. "See you around, then," she said.

"If we don't all die within the next two hours," he replied.

"Don't think that way," she chided. "For all we know, the Darkness might take one look at us and decide it's not worth it."

"Yeah, right," he snorted.

"You're too negative."

"Think of it this way," he explained. "I have a wife and two kids to take care of, and we might all die before I get home from work."

"I change my mind," she decided. "We might all die in the next two hours."

Muddywings charged in, startling the both of them. "Airgor told me you were in here," she panted. "Ace just passed out! What do we do now?"

"Who?" Rocky asked confusedly.

"Never mind," Jade answered. "We really need to get someone else, though."

"What kind of person are you looking for?" Rocky asked.

"A creature who is strong in the mind-term," Muddywings explained. "Do you know anybody with that qualification?"

"I took meditation school for a while," he replied. "Does that count?"

Jade and Muddywings looked at each other.

"Well," Jade said. "How do you feel about raising the dead?"

Chapter Sixteen:
And Then the Earth Shook

It was clear that Rocky wasn't sure he'd heard her correctly. He dug his paw into his ears as if cleaning out wax. "Sorry, what was that?"

"We need you to say a spell and animate some ancient corpses of creatures from previous wars," Jade explained. "It's for the good of the Kingdom of Imagination."

He gave her and Muddywings a look like, *Why did I say that I took meditation school?*

"Fine," he relented. "I just hope this isn't a long-term thing."

"Don't worry, it shouldn't be," Muddywings assured him. "You just need to hurry. SWOOP!" she roared suddenly. "GET DOWN TO THE NEWSROOM RIGHT NOW!"

A loud crash from above, probably because someone flew into a wall. Moments later, Swoop bolted in. "Yes? Yes," he said.

"Do you have him on speed dial or something?" Jade wondered.

"Please explain to Rocky the spell for awakening the dead," Muddywings told Swoop, ignoring Jade. "And then show him the room we've been using."

"Okay," Swoop responded. "Come on. You've got a lot of work to do."

Rocky nervously followed Swoop out of the newsroom.

"We should probably check on Ace," Jade said.

"You're right," Muddywings agreed. "I sort of just left him there."

They raced back down to the dungeons (yes, more running; Jade felt like her legs were turning to marshmallow filling). Ace was slumped on the cold gray floor. Three dragonish creatures were blinking around confusedly.

One looked like she had orange spotlights for eyes and a miniature black ball with a golden glow around it for a tail.

Another one was swamp green and had webbing between his claws. He looked sort of like an alligator, with her long, rounded snout and little flaps down her spine.

The third had silvery-white scales. Her claws looked like they were covered in barbed wires, probably for walking on ice. She had a ball of ice on her tail. The back of each foot had a little hook, maybe in case one of her kind fell off a glacier.

"What in the name of Anivia is going on?" demanded the glowing dragon. "I'm out in the middle of a battle, and suddenly, I'm here."

"I agree with her," the white dragon added. "Why is everything in my mind so *blank*? Who are you?" She pointed to Jade. "Why are you wearing Peacebringer's Crown?"

"That can't be," Muddywings objected. "That went missing centuries ago."

"It disappeared when the Darkness came," she argued.

"First of all, what are your names and what kind of creature are you?" Jade interjected.

"I'm Snowflake," said the white dragon. "I'm an Ice Dragon."

"My name is Dawnmoon, and I'm an Eclipse Dragon," replied the glowing dragon.

"And my name is Craggerdil," responded the green dragon. "I am a Swamp Dragon."

"Okay," Jade said briskly. "Ace the Cheetahphant over there brought you back from the dead to help fight the Darkness. Make sense?"

"No," said the three dragons in unison.

"Basically, we need your help to protect the Kingdom of Imagination from being utterly destroyed," Muddywings summed up. "Do you still remember how to fight?"

"Can a fish swim? Of *course* we can still fight," snorted Dawnmoon. "Why wouldn't we be able to?"

"Well, then, let's go! There's an attack about to happen, and we've hardly prepared at all!" Muddywings growled. "Come on! There are some more of you guys in the dungeon down the hall on the left. Move it!"

"Are you a descendant of General Talonstreak?" Craggerdil asked Muddywings. "You look exactly like him."

"And you sound exactly like him," Snowflake commented.

"Probably," Muddywings responded. "But this is no time to stand around and chitchat! There is a *war* about to happen here!"

"All right, all right!" Craggerdil grumbled. "Let's go, guys."

"Jade, could you please go get the other *Wamekufa*?" Muddywings prompted her.

"Sure," Jade replied.

She raced out of the room and into the other dungeon. Dozens of creatures sat there talking quietly. They looked up when she entered the room.

"Come on, everybody," she said to all the creatures. "If you still have questions, they can be answered later. Right now, we have to get prepared for an attack. Follow me."

Without question, every creature stood and trotted after her as she went back up to the ground level rooms.

Jade led them towards the armory, which was near the main courtyard in the center of Imagination Castle. The main weapon smith took one look at the crowd and ran to the back room where most of the weapons and armor was stored. She came back with a chariot full of gear and a squadron of creatures in tow.

The main weapon smith had two horse legs, a golden turtle shell, human hands, and the head of a bird. She was covered in ashes from working to create new armor and weapons.

"Hi," she greeted Jade. "I'm Kaia, a Hooved Turtle Bird. Let me guess—soldiers preparing for battle? Because if that's the case, we've been working on some pretty sweet enchanted weapons."

The pile of weapons consisted of glowing swords, bows with spell writing on them, spears cracking with power…. It was like a magical array of deadly killing objects.

"Yes, these guys need to get armor and weapons," Jade said. "Thanks."

"All right," Kaia decided. "Let's do this. Monkshood, you cover the dragons. Barracuda, you suit up the water creatures. Jojo, you arm the winged creatures. Aikazax, you handle the little guys. I'll get the rest of them."

Monkshood was a light green dragon with dark green vines with little leaves all over him. The vines swirled all over his scales.

Barracuda had the body of a ninja larnternshark, the tail of a barracuda, and little ridges all down his spine. He was encased in a water sphere, which confused Jade, since he worked in a weapon shop that required its employees to use fire. Maybe it was magic, which made a lot of sense.

Jojo was a Wollion. She had the biggest forepaws Jade had ever seen in her entire time being here. She had light gray fur, probably representing the wolf in her. The tip of her tail had a patch of black skin. Jade guessed she had a little accident in the forges: She had been innocently hammering a hot sword when someone decided to make lots of sparks fly.

Or she was innocently hammering a hot sword and not realized her tail had caught fire.

Aikazax was about as big as Jade's hand. He had three centipede legs on each side, a bee stinger on the tip of his tail, a bird beak, and wings.

"You should probably go check on our other soldiers," Muddywings said to Jade. "I'll make sure everybody gets geared up."

"Thanks," Jade replied. "I'll do that."

She left the armory, cut through a couple other courtyards, got lost in the labyrinth-like halls, and ended up about a quarter of a mile away from her destination. Luckily, a thirty-foot-tall giraffe-like guard found her wandering around and pointed her in the right direction.

When she finally reached the training camp, she was astonished by what she saw. The place was swarming with new and old recruits. Most of them were sparring. The others were cleaning weapons, fitting armor, and sharpening claws. A couple winged creatures were practicing air combat together.

A gigantic, armored creature with the body of a snake, human arms, and two bird heads with wings on the sides slithered up to her. "Greetings, Queen Jade," he said. "I am General Kamkhasthingat, a Double-Headed Bird Snake. I command the Fifth Imperial Squadron. Is there anything I can do for you?"

"General...um, how do you pronounce your name again?"

"Kamkhasthingat...you can call me General K. Everyone does," he replied.

"How are they doing?" Jade asked him, nodding towards a couple Bi-Mouth Tri-Ocular Dragicorns were arguing over who stole whose poker money.

"They're excellent fighters," General Kamkhasthingat responded. "Even the new recruits are learning fast. It's probably because of the fact they're about to be attacked, and they want to be as trained as possible."

A big shadow fell over Jade. She looked up. Circling down on her was Meadow.

Meadow hardly made marks the ground with her claws as she lightly landed. "Hi," she wheezed. "Howler's on his way! We're so worried!"

"We should be fine," Jade replied.

"That's not reassuring," Meadow snorted. "That 'should' should not be in there."

"But then it would just be 'We be fine'. That doesn't make any sense at all."

While they were talking, Jade let her senses down. Something large and extremely furry bowled her over. It was Howler.

"Hello, Jade," he puffed. "So, do you think we can survive this attack?"

Jade thought for a moment. "If the Darkness has as big of an army as the one I saw in my dreams, then I'd say we have a seventy percent chance of death."

"Thanks a lot for that low-spirit approximation," Howler grumbled. "By the way, what dreams are you talking about?"

"Oh, right!" Jade felt embarrassed. "I forgot to tell you two, didn't I?"

"Yep," Meadow confirmed.

"Try not to keep important things like that away from your best friends," Howler added. "We're a team, in case you haven't figured it out yet. No secrets!"

"Don't worry, I have," Jade assured him. "Anyway, about the dreams... Anivia sent them to me to warn me about the Darkness. Gredra turned some good creatures evil, and their army grew very large in a very short amount of time."

"What creatures?" Meadow inquired.

"Well, there's Whitecap the Deer-Footed Elephant Shark, Sunbolt the Sugar Glider Bird, Heavenfeather the Spiked Unicorn Dird, Strongkick the Lock Ness Osritch, Coral the Loch Ness Monster, Monkey the Long-Tailed Lemur Bird, Crescent the Vampire Moon Dragon, Abalone the Pterodactyl Eel, Buzz the Fanged Butterfly Hornet, and Hora the Wollion," Jade answered.

"H-h-hora?" Howler asked.

"Yes," Jade replied. "Why? Isn't that the missing Wollion you were talking about earlier when we came out of the tunnels of Tormakk Rock?"

"Yes, I mean, I just wanted to know if she was fine." Howler seemed really agitated.

"If 'fine' means you've been turned evil and are serving the Darkness, then she's perfect," Jade responded.

Howler shuddered. "Please, no more of this description," he whimpered.

"Besides, we should probably get some armor and weapons," Meadow suggested. "We don't want to be caught in the middle of a battle with no defense."

"All I need is armor." Howler flexed his claws. "These are my weapons."

"And I can't exactly hold a weapon," Meadow added.

"And I can create my own weapons and armor," Jade told them. "I know how to use Lunar Twilight Magic."

"Ooh, really?" Meadow wondered. "I heard it's incredibly hard, and that only Royals can actually do it."

"I've also heard of Lunar Twilight Magic," General Kamkhasthingat interrupted. "That's completely wicked!"

"Can you show us?" Howler asked curiously.

"All right," Jade decided. "However, it might take a while."

Howler sat down and wrapped his tail around his tail patiently.

Jade let her senses spread through the ground, searching for the jades she used to connect with Lunar Twilight Magic. Way deep down, she found a clump of the green rocks in a cave system right next to a small patch of diamonds. The earth rumbled.

The jades burst through the ground. They hovered and melted together, forming armor, a shield, and a sword in a sheath that automatically attached itself to her.

"Wow," Meadow chirped.

"Amazing," General Kamkhasthingat exclaimed.

"That is insane," Howler summed up. "I wonder if you can make some for us...."

Boom. Golden dust rained down from the golden wall of invincible thorns. Jade looked up and saw weird cracks spreading through the sky. All around, soldiers glanced up as if it was a skyquake instead of an earthquake.

Boom. Crack! The dome shattered and chunks of rock fell from the sky like meteors.

The army of Dark Creatures had begun the attack.

Chapter Seventeen:
Killing a V.I.P. --- a Very Idiotic Penguin

Dark clouds appeared. They were strangely large and sudden.

Wait a second, Jade thought. *Those are not clouds. Those are Dark Creatures, and they're trying to destroy the Kingdom of Imagination, not make it drizzle.*

That made her mad. She hadn't been Queen for very long, yet there was already a war trying to happen.

"Troops!" General Kamkhasthingat roared. "Prepare to attack!"

The camp was suddenly extremely busy. Soldiers hastily grabbed weapons off racks and began lining up in Attack Formation Tiger (it was clearly a known tactic). Had they been slightly more prepared, this would not have happened!

Jade's brain processed what happened next slowly. The army of Dark Creatures was the size of how big the sun looked. All of a sudden, like the Big Bang, everything expanded. The sky was completely blotted out.

Dragons and birdlike creatures launched themselves into the air. The rest of the soldiers swarmed the ground, like a mob of angry, well-armed dangerous, mixed-up animals.

The army of Dark Creatures did not like the fact that the Kingdom of Imagination had an army that could fight. They had no mercy, either. They attacked so viciously Jade wondered how the dragons with ripped wings were still flying.

Blood showered from above while more blood watered the ground. There were different types of blood, too: black blood, white blood, red blood, blue blood, and some strange green blood that no one seemed to want to touch.

A squad of Dark Creatures cut Jade, Howler, and Meadow off from General Kamkhasthingat. The black animals were closing in from every direction, including the air. One made the mistake of attempting to spear Meadow. Her wing was only lightly grazed, but she squawked in anger and pecked him on the head.

Howler took that as a sign of *attack now*. He launched himself at the nearest Dark Creature, which happened to be an all-bone giant wolf. The wolf outsized him, but it didn't matter. Howler may have been smaller, but he was smarter. He hit a pressure point on the skeletal wolf's bone, which prevented it from attacking for a few more moments. He used this to snap off a rib.

Meadow caused a lot of havoc by flapping her wings in her attacker's faces. It turns out *Plathai* wings hurt as much as chicken wings when flapped hard enough. She also ripped off fur with her talons and caused headaches and head wounds with her beak, as it was very sharp. Also, her bright, flowery tail could do some serious damage by making her enemies go 'Ooh, pretty!', so she could peck them to death. Also, she could make her tail release such an exotic smell that everyone wanted to get close.

That left Jade with the biggest of them all: a large black penguin thing with several sets of blades for arms and breathed ice (because it wouldn't make sense for a creature that lived in the cold to breathe fire).

Knife Penguin charged. Luckily for Jade, giant penguins weren't accustomed to waddling uphill on a field slick with blood. It was more like a treadmill set too fast. However, just because its arms couldn't reach her didn't mean its stupid ice-breath wouldn't. It stopped struggling up the slope, drew in a large gulp of air, and belched it back out on a wave of cold.

Jade dove to one side. She looked to where the ice-breath had landed. It had completely frozen one of Meadow's attackers.

Well, Jade decided, *better not get hit. I don't want to hurt him, but he's trying to kill me. So I should probably kill him first.*

She had survived the first bit, but now she was at the same level as Knife Penguin. He barreled towards her, blade arms outstretched. She raised her glowing shield just in time, but it still felt like getting hit by a charging bull.

Blades were spinning all around her, trying to get under her shield. Thank Anivia that it was large enough to cover her. Suddenly, the weight disappeared. Howler had taken a break from the half-paralyzed Bone Wolf and had come over to help.

Her reinforcement did not have a long rest time. Bone Wolf was soon back on her skeletal paws and attacking again.

Jade scrambled to her feet, only to have blades thrust towards her again. This time, she blocked with her shield and stabbed Knife Penguin with her sword. He let out another wave of ice-breath, low enough to jump over. She guessed that he was trying to freeze her feet so she couldn't move.

Except it spreads, she thought. *In which case, he is just trying to kill me.*

When Knife Penguin used ice-breath again, she got less lucky. The frost had completely covered her shield and had almost reached her hand before she realized she should drop it. Now she was completely shieldless.

Knife Penguin used his blades. Somehow, Jade managed to maneuver long enough to not die and put herself between the arms and Knife Penguin. As soon as he jabbed another arm, she ducked down. The blade went right into his gut. Screeching, he tried again. Another one sliced at her legs. She jumped. He stabbed himself in the crotch. Knife Penguin was committing suicide.

He attempted to kill her once more. As she straightened up, he aimed for her head. She swerved just in time. With a wail, Knife Penguin stabbed himself in the heart. Toppling over, he almost fell on top of Jade.

She wondered why he didn't just use ice-breath. Maybe he didn't want to accidentally freeze his blades off. Her thinking was cut short when an Earth Dragon crash-landed right next to her, belly shredded. Now was not the time to ponder on why penguins were so stupid.

Jade glanced around. Howler was still fighting Bone Wolf, who was missing a couple body parts. Meadow was bleeding and out of tricks. She had taken down two of her attackers, minus the one that got turned into a Popsicle, but three more remained.

Jade dashed over to her friend, who was currently cornered. Sneaking up on a Snag, she diced a pair of legs. Too bad it had screamed and alerted the others to her presence.

While Jade distracted them, Meadow made her great escape by taking off and flying into a brick wall. She still accomplished liftoff after, though. Swooping back around, she dive-bombed one of the creatures who had a dragon body, head, and wings, as well as two other heads: a goat and a cobra. He only looked mildly annoyed from her pecks and launched into the air, chasing her.

The last Dark Creature was pitifully small. She had dragon wings, a dragon snout, and a dragon tail, but she had no legs and her body was the size of a ping-pong ball.

Small Dragon could still breathe fire. Jade found that out right when she raised her sword. A burst of flame shot from Small Dragon's snout. The flame was also very small, and she had no problem dodging it. While doing so, Jade smacked Small Dragon with the flat side of her blade. Small Dragon went flying into some bushes, where she did not move.

Howler had finally finished off Bone Wolf and helped Meadow with Weird Hydra by grabbing the biggest bone from Bone Wolf and hurling it upward. It hit Weird Hydra's wing, causing him to fall. Once he landed, Howler made a big deal of ripping out all of his windpipes and eating his heart.

"Ew," Meadow panted as she touched the ground. "Can't you do that after?"

Howler didn't reply to that specific question, but he did say, "Come on. Let's go find some more bad guys to kill."

They didn't have to wait long for another Dark Creature to come wandering along. Actually, there wasn't just one. There were so many the three became separated.

A jackal-headed snake lead a squadron of Dark Creatures towards her. Some creature's venomous tail stabbed downwards at her face. Unexpectedly, it was chopped off before it reached her.

A dark green dragon with two tails that looked equally venomous as the one that had tried to kill her swooped in with a squadron of his own. "Go home, you scale-brained horror frogs!" he roared. "Go home or we'll turn you into the remains of a kamikaze ant!"

Battle burst out all around Jade. An overlarge wingless wasp crawled towards her, two creatures that slightly resembled serpopards from Egyptian mythology flanking it. The serpopard-things had necks as long as a giraffe's, fangs like a baboon, and a single snake for tails.

Serpopard-Thing Number One couldn't wait to get killing. She barreled forward like a steam engine, neck outstretched for an earlier bite.

Wow, Jade thought. *They are* really *stupid.*

As soon as Serpopard-Thing Number One's head was in range, Jade sidestepped and slashed out with her sword, cutting her head not-so-cleanly off. The snake tail was still wriggling, so she sliced that off, too.

Serpopard-Thing Number Two clearly learned from Serpopard-Thing Number One's mistakes. He advanced slower. He lashed out suddenly, feinting an aim at her legs.

Then, his tail bit her hand as hard as its little mouth could bite. The wound didn't seem venomous, but she couldn't be sure.

While she was dealing with the snake, Serpopard-Thing Number Two clenched his teeth onto her sword arm. Yellow spots danced in front of her eyes. The next thing she knew, she was disarmed and lying flat on the ground with Serpopard-Thing Number Two's fangs inches away from her throat.

Suddenly, a massive gray shape leaped onto Serpopard-Thing Number Two. Growling, the stranger herded Serpopard-Thing Number Two back. An oversized wolf, her fangs were twice as long as a Serpopard-Thing's. Her paws were as large as dinner plates. Any self-respecting non-idiotic creature would flee in terror when they saw her stalking them.

Serpopard-Thing Number Two, however, was an idiot. He growled right back at her, as well as looked her in the eye. Jade had learned in science class that dogs were descendants from wolves, and wolves tended to attack whoever looked them in the eye.

Giant Wolf ran past Serpopard-Thing Number Two, shredding his hide with her claws as she went by. Serpopard-Thing Number Two tried to turn and attack her tail, but Giant Wolf was on the other side of him.

As Giant Wolf was fighting, Wingless Wasp was creeping upon her, stinger ready. Jade tried to yell warning, but her voice was weak for some reason. Instead, she picked up her sword with the hand the snake had bitten and spun it like a Frisbee as hard as she could towards Wingless Wasp.

Jade had never been good at Frisbee, but this time, luck was on her side. Her sword hit true, hitting the tail and then somehow was directed down to Wingless Wasp's neck. He found out he no longer had a head.

Meanwhile, Serpopard-Thing Number Two had both of his throats slit and was lying in a puddle of blood. Giant Wolf was busy with another enemy. However, this enemy was too powerful for even her. Giant Wolf soon perished.

Jade retrieved her sword, which was covered in amber-colored goo. No sooner had she done that, than she saw a creature with a lion's body, bull horns, and a snake for a tail (yes, more snakes) standing a half a mile away on a hill.

He was not alone. Behind him stood at least a two dozen more of his kind. She guessed that they would cause a stampede and rip her into a pile of Bull Chow. However much she hated killing magical creatures, she most definitely did not want to become dinner for a bunch of herbivores.

The herd of Lion Cows charged. They picked up speed quickly. Jade was left with a choice: Run or die.

As they neared, the leader tried as hard as he could to slam on the brakes. Something caught Jade's eye from both sides.

A whole pride/crash of Rhinolions were charging down another hill behind Jade. She recognized Meerkat, Savannah, Cleptora, and of course, Chief Loki.

The herd of Lion Cows may have looked strong before, but even the largest of bulls are no match for so many rhinoceroses.

"RUN AWAY!" the leader of the herd yelled.

The Rhinolions were quicker. The battle gave the terms "fur flying" and "bloodbath" new meanings. With all of the blood raining down, and all of the blood coming off of creatures around her, she appeared to have been dunked in some very strange shades of watercolor.

The arrival of the Rhinolions was not the only good news. Illuminati had survived and was fighting back to back with her.

Jade was in the middle of a fight with a winged polar bear when he arrived. Illuminati saw her and instantly drove his horn right into Flying Bear's thigh. He pulled it out and finished the process of dying Flying Bear's fur bright red.

"Thanks," she gasped. Since her fight with Serpopard-Thing Number Two, she had been slower and gotten many more injuries from Flying Bear and friends.

"No problem," he replied. "Are you planning on getting some sword-fighting lessons? You look like you could use those."

"There is *nothing* wrong with my fighting techniques." Jade gritted her teeth; the pain of battle was getting to her.

"Do your fighting techniques include being shredded into a pile of horse poop?" he asked, tilting his head. "Because if it is, it is certainly working."

"Shut up."

"You're right. We still have to win."

Together they fought their way through countless hordes of enemies. Occasionally, a friend or ally would show up for long enough to help kill a Dark Creature, but they soon vanished in the mess, some turning up dead later on in the battle.

As Jade was fighting, she lost track of her dragonish friend. An angry roar behind her made her turn.

There, in the death grip of an evil dragon, was Illuminati.

Chapter Eighteen:
Saved by a Magic Hat

"J-j-jade," Illuminati stuttered. "Watch-"

She realized that he was trying to warn her. Whipping around, she was face-to-face with a crocodile with a stinger and venomous teeth.

"Oh, do not worry about your friend," he chuckled. "He'll make a fine addition to our army. As for you, we make no promises. We have been given direct orders to kill the Queen."

A pitch-black Oasis Bird hopped forward with an axe in his talons.

"Goodbye, Queen of the Kingdom of Imagination," he rumbled, bringing down the axe onto Jade's face.

Had it not been for her magic hat, Jade wouldn't have reacted fast enough to defend herself. Only the hat kept her alive.

The coiled-up golden Ridgeback Rattlesnake on her head sprung to life, lunging faster than people to the shops on Black Friday. It bit onto the Oasis Bird's talon so hard he was forced to drop the axe in mid swing, which clattered onto Venom Croc's foot, taking off several toes.

Venom Croc screamed. Jade's crown-snake coiled itself on her head again and turned back into a pretty work of art.

She turned to the dragon that held Illuminati captive. "Let him go or I'll turn you and your friends into the remains of a kamikaze ant!" she snarled.

Most of Bad Dragon's allies turned and fled, leaving only him and two others. Bad Dragon just threw back his head (which was probably empty) and laughed.

"Little girl, do you think I can be imitated enough into letting scale-brain here go?" he growled. "Attempt one thing, and we'll kill...OW!"

Bad Dragon thrashed his tail around until something came flying off. Another Bi-Mouth Tri-Ocular Dragicorn had bitten the tip of his tail.

She stood up. "*No one* holds my son hostage and gets away with it," she hissed.

Oh, Jade thought. *This must be Illuminati's mom.*

Illuminati's mom drew herself up higher and roared, "Fellow Bi-Mouth Tri-Ocular Dragicorns, attack!"

Six more Bi-Mouth Tri-Ocular Dragicorns appeared. They bellowed and charged.

Bad Dragon's eyes widened in shock and pain as two Dragicorns rammed their horns into his gut. They tugged them out and started the process of using both of their snouts to get through more thick dragon scales, Illuminati not far behind them.

Bad Dragon's friends weren't doing so good, either. One was already dead and the other was coming close. Soon, all three were lying in a puddle of various shades of blood.

"Illuminati!" his mother gasped. "Are you all right? Are you hurt?" She kissed him firmly on the head with both snouts.

"Relax, Mom." He rolled his eyes. "Other than having just been in a fight, I'm fine."

Another Bi-Mouth Tri-Ocular Dragicorn wove between them. "We should get going," he warned, "or we'll either be picked off or surrounded."

He had a point; they were at the bottom of a valley, sides rising up all around them.

"Let's head for where the fighting is worst," Jade suggested.

Illuminati's mother tuned towards her. "You want to go where the battle is awful?" she asked. "Where we could all easily die? Because if that's the case, we're in. We want to serve our Kingdom the best."

"All right," Jade replied. "Let's go."

"How will we know where fighting is worst?" one Dragicorn asked.

"We'll hear it," she responded. "What are your names?"

"I'm Dsasrett," answered the Dragicorn who had asked about where the fighting was.

"I'm Emeraldscales," said one.

"My name is Amatheon," growled another.

"I am Night," snarled Illuminati's mom. "Can we get moving so we can slowly torture the army of Dark Creatures?"

"And I'm Ngumu-mfupa," finished a big male. "Let's go teach these scale-brained horror frog-looking gallons of hagfish slime a lesson."

Jade didn't know exactly what a horror frog or hagfish was, but it sounded pretty bad.

The seven of them took off up the slope. After about a mile, Jade began to fall behind. Emeraldscales slowed her pace to match hers.

"Do you want a ride?" she asked, sympathy in her eyes. "We usually run very fast, and your wounds don't seem to be helping."

"Okay," Jade agreed.

The others waited while Jade scrambled onto Emeraldscales' back. Then, they were back to running through the Kingdom.

It wasn't hard to find the biggest battle. Screeches of pain echoed through the air. Roars of anger reverberated of walls and cliffs. Blood was everywhere. Fur, feathers, and scales littered the ground like disgusting confetti. And the bodies...there were bodies everywhere. Those were all clues to where everyone had gone.

The Bi-Mouth Tri-Ocular Dragicorns charged straight into battle, Jade still riding Emeraldscales like she was in the Kentucky Rodeo.

The scene was worse than expected. Imagine walking onto a battlefield during World War II. Now stop imagining because it was three thousand times as bad as that. Jade hoped she looked fearsome, riding her deadly unicorn friend into battle and waving her glowing green sword like a maniac.

A swarm of small house cat-sized winged tigers engulfed them. They bit and clawed Emeraldscales, so she bit and clawed them right back. Jade stuck to swinging her sword around until she hit something.

Both of them were looking pretty battered after that, but they didn't have time to rest. A few deer-footed elephant creatures approached them.

Elephant Deer Number One and Two bellowed and instantly barreled towards them. Emeraldscales swiftly dodged to one side. Elephant Deer Number One plowed into a tree. Elephant Deer Number Two accidentally stomped on several allies, sparing some Kingdom creatures from slow and painful death.

Elephant Deer Number One righted herself and charged with Elephant Deer Number Three at her side. Elephant Deer Number Two had gotten into some trouble with Wollions and was busy dying.

Emeraldsclales darted in between both of the Elephant Deer, destroying Number Three's thick hide while Jade scraped her sword along Number One's. Elephant Deer Number One and Three both turned inward, colliding into each other. They were going to have headaches for a while, if they survived the battle.

A large white rabbit with blood red eyes, wings, and chicken feet galloped towards them. At first, Jade thought it was another enemy, but Chicken Bunny simply leaped over their heads and attacked a herd of various hooved creatures. She looked alone until a colony of bats with pig faces and feet followed.

A dark green dragon with ram horns and the snout, fangs, and paws of a sabretooth tiger snarled at them. Luckily, a friendly flying fox (no joke, it was an actual winged fox, not a type of bat) was nearby and had the time to help out.

Flying Fox landed on Ram Dragon and snapped at his wings so he couldn't escape. Jade and Emeraldcales dashed around his feet, stabbing and biting his legs.

Ram Dragon swiped at Jade and Emeraldscales. The blow connected, sending them soaring. Flying Fox was thrown off.

Flying Fox tuned to them. "You guys sneak around and attack from behind," she ordered. "I'll distract him."

Jade nodded. "I'll go left, you go right," she told Emeraldscales.

"And I'll signal with my tail for attack," Flying Fox added.

They sidled around while Flying Fox yelled insults at Ram Dragon.

"You're a blob fish-faced piece of pygmy sperm whale poop!" she taunted. "Son of a poacher! Scale-brain! Vulture breath!"

Jade and Emeraldscales had made it around to the back of Ram Dragon. Spotting them, Flying Fox raised her tail high and slammed it down: the sign for attack.

They ran towards Ram Dragon. Jade leaped onto his back and grabbed onto his wings to balance herself. Emeraldscales attacked his tail, as it was apparently a weak spot for dragons.

She slashed at Ram Dragon's thick scales. She only made scratches, but it still worked. Flying Fox also joined in. Ram Dragon now had three different enemies from three different sides.

Within a couple minutes, Ram Dragon was dead. But then a whole lot of large creatures with only skin, crab claws, and fangs like razors charged in. Two more creatures joined in to help them. One was an elk with wings and the other was a flaming cheetah.

Super Elk flew around banging into Skin Crabs while Fire Cheetah lived up to her name by lighting them up. Flying Fox attacked one and Emeraldscales double-bit another. Jade helped by getting thrown, landing on the back of one, and chopping his head off.

Throwing things seemed to be the main weapon of the Skin Crabs, which made no sense because they had claws instead of hands. Emeraldscales also got launched and landed face-first in a tree. She scrabbled out and attacked again.

Jade dodged in and out of range. Occasionally she would get tossed into the air. Every time, she would attempt to land on another Skin Crab's head. Sometimes it worked, and she relieved a Skin Crab of his or her head. Other times it didn't work and she would get trampled by one of them.

A Skin Crab pinned her down and raised his big claw in the air, about to bash her skull in. But Jade had more tricks up her sleeve. She went limp, and the Skin Crab released her in surprise. She grabbed onto her magic sword with both hands and cut open Skin Crab from gut to chin.

The five of them worked well together. They soon became used to each other's tricks. Super Elk liked to dive in and then get out. Fire Cheetah relied on strength and dried leaves. Flying Fox was all about being sneaky (as foxes usually are). Emeraldscales used her three eyes, sharp horn, pointy tail, and two mouths to her advantage.

Seven more creatures ended up with them. They all had giraffe bodies and necks, as well as cat tails, heads, and feet. They fought as hard as the Skin Crabs.

Now they outnumbered the enemy. Soon, the rest of the Skin Crabs were either dead or dying slowly and painfully. The Giraffe Cats only had minor injuries, but the others were bleeding in at least ten different places. It was good to have fresh reinforcements.

More Dark Creatures approached them. Two were big, bug like, spiky, and had wings. One was a snake with a cat head. Three were small butterflies with fangs and wings that made a skull face. Five were horrifying human-looking creatures with wings for arms, bird feet, and red eyes. All eleven were mad.

Jade raised her sword. Fire Cheetah and Flying Fox growled. Emeraldscales snapped her two jaws and waved her devil tail menacingly. Super Elk tossed his head. The Giraffe Cats hissed. Total, there were twelve of them, but that didn't mean they would beat the eleven equally dangerous Dark Creatures.

The Dark Creatures charged. Most of them were fairly fast and left some of the others behind. The Big Bugs were really good at jumping. One landed on top of a Giraffe Cat and they went tumbling off into the bushes, where yowls and bug-smashing happened. The other landed in front of Jade.

Big Bug looked even uglier up close. He rammed his spikes into Jade. She was tossed into the air. She would have landed onto more spikes, but a golden shape flashed underneath her, knocking Big Bug out of the way.

It was Howler.

"Howler!" she wheezed. "How did you find us?"

"I followed your scent," he replied, not taking his eyes off of the spot where Big Bug lay unmoving. "Also, I figured you'd head to where the fighting was worst."

"You guessed right," Jade gasped. The spikes had scored deep wounds.

"I'm here, too," Meadow chirped from a tree.

"Stay up there," Howler called. "I don't want you to get...."

A dark shape tackled him. They tussled for a few seconds, biting and clawing. Before Jade could rush in to help, Howler let out a roar of pain. The black figure got off, turned, and bounded away.

But Jade still recognized who it was...Hora.

She and Meadow rushed to Howler's side. There was a bad wound in his neck, as well as several puncture wounds in his belly.

"No, no, *no*," Meadow fretted. "Howler, please wake up."

"Come on, Howler." Jade gritted her teeth. The physical pain was too much; she couldn't bear mental pain as well. "Wake *up*. I order you not to die. Come back and rule the Wollions."

She knew it wouldn't work. There was a sort of dullness in his pupils that kept growing, spreading like cancer.

And then the light faded out of her friend's eyes forever.

Epilogue

Amatheon was having a really bad day.

He had gotten separated from the others, almost had his stomach ripped out, had been hit on the head by a coconut—*a mystery as to where it even came from*—had been drowned by an evil swamp creature uglier than a blob fish with an eye infection, and was back for more.

Now he stood facing off with some weird mix of a buffalo, a viper, and a jaguar. He had spotted fur, a snakelike tail, a forked tongue, reptilian eyes, fangs, large horns, hooves for hind legs, and claws for front legs. Even stranger, he was a normal color, not a part of the Army of Dark Creatures.

Buffalo-Viper-Jaguar growled, his two eyes boring into Amatheon's three.

"What's wrong with you?" Amatheon yelped. "You know you're fighting on the wrong side, right? I'm a good guy."

Buffalo-Viper-Jaguar made a sound like a hyena. "I chose my side. The Darkness is stronger than any kid Queen could be. If you want to be noble, stick with the losing team and find out what happens to those who oppose the Darkness. Join now, and your life shall be spared."

"Tempting," Amatheon replied. "But I've got something you don't have. I actually have a brain, not a sorry excuse of one that's smaller than a fairyfly." And with that, he launched himself in the general direction of Mr. Confident.

Buffalo-Viper-Jaguar easily dodged. Amatheon landed on the ground and felt a jolt of pain shoot through his leg. He realized there was a hole filled with roots that his claw had fallen into, and he couldn't get it free.

The traitor whipped around, lowered his horns, and took off at a gallop. He collided with Amatheon, who was still trapped.

One horn missed Amatheon's neck by about half an inch. The other went straight into his shoulder. He screamed as blood ran down his scales and watered the ground.

With a wrench, Buffalo-Viper-Jaguar removed his horn from Amatheon's flesh. "I gave you a choice," he rumbled. "You chose wrong."

Amatheon managed to free himself from the hole and turned towards his opponent, but he was too late. Two horns hit his chest, shattering his rib cage and poking holes in his heart and lungs. Life was ripped from his very body, and Amatheon collapsed, dead.

. . . . .

Reaper the Wollion hated battle. He hated dying. He hated taking lives. Ironic. His mother should've waited to see what kind of cub he would be before naming him.

Right now, he was in the shadow of Ruby Castle, fighting a black Horned Lionsnake, and trying very hard not to die. It wasn't working out. He'd already been roasted by a Fire Boar and didn't want to repeat the experience.

Suddenly, something changed. There was something in the air, and it definitely wasn't love. It had a sort of *wrong* to it. Everyone around him froze and looked towards Ruby Castle. Reaper used the distraction to his advantage and tackled the Horned Lionsnake. They tussled for a moment before Reaper pushed her over the edge of Jackdaw Cliff.

Sorry, he thought guiltily. Then he turned to look at the Castle.

A cheer erupted from the Army of Dark Creatures. "We have won!" they shouted. "Hail the Darkness!"

As they were celebrating, an inky blackness crept out of a window on the seventh floor. This, Reaper knew, was the Darkness.

And then it spoke. "Surrender. Kneel before me. Kneel, and your life shall be spared."

The Army of Dark Creatures immediately knelt. The remaining defenders of the Kingdom did not try to strike, for they knew that they would surely be killed.

Time to choose, Reaper thought. *Betray everyone and everything that I've ever known, or fight back for what is right. Or you can jump over Jackdaw Cliff. There's water...no guarantee of living. Judging by the height, I just might....* He did some quick calculations. *There is a way to survive. But whatever you choose, you need to choose* now.

And with that, Reaper leaped over the edge of the cliff, plummeting to what was almost certain death. *Better than the other options,* he thought while trying to quickly maneuver his way toward the lake.

He landed on the water, all right. It crushed almost every bone in his body on impact.

Made in the USA
Columbia, SC
20 April 2018